RUNNIN… OD
PRA… –
R… KE

C… shot down the…
'Slow… wee screamed, 'we comin… !'
Wendell… down, but not much. Thank God the planks were in place! They bounced on, weaving crazily from side to side. The sound of gunfire faded, and Wendell began to enjoy himself. He was a real, no-shit bootlegger now, and the fastest thing on wheels. He speeded up, though the turns were coming faster and sharper. 'C'mon, Peewee, stop fretting,' he said, 'I been on these roads once, that's all I need.' His voice was calm, as if he were just taking his grandma out for a Sunday drive, as the car ran down into a ditch on one side of the road and right back up again. Peewee slumped clear down on the floor and lay curled up under the dashboard. He seemed to be praying . . .

Greased Lightning

KEN VOSE AND LARRY DUKORE

SPHERE BOOKS LIMITED
30/32 Gray's Inn Road, London WC1X 8JL

First published in Great Britain by Sphere Books Ltd. 1977

TRADE
MARK

Set in Intertype Baskerville

Printed in Great Britain by
Hunt Barnard Printing Ltd.,
Aylesbury, Bucks.

EDITOR'S NOTE

Wendell Scott still lives in Danville, Virginia. He has been semi-retired from racing competition since he was involved in a crash, at more than one hundred and fifty miles an hour, at Talladega, Alabama, in 1973. By then he had raced nearly one thousand times and logged more than 72,000 miles in Grand National competition alone. During the filming of *Greased Lightning*, he served as technical advisor to ensure the accuracy of the racing sequences and drove in all of them. He also built replicas of some of the cars he drove during the period treated by the film.

BOOK I

I

The bus from Newport News to Roanoke was only a half-hour behind schedule, but it seemed like it was never going to make it to Danville. Stretched sleepily out in the back of the bus, Wendell Scott gave up all hope for the sharp creases in his sweat-soaked khakis. Jesus, but it was hot! Up front, the few white passengers nodded. Even with the windows open, the dust motes swirled slowly, and the air was like a blast furnace.

Shit, thought Wendell, bus gets any slower and I'll get out and push. From where he sprawled, it looked like the driver was asleep, too. Might as well be, for all the speed they were making. Oh, the hell with it! he decided. He wadded up his Eisenhower jacket and put it under his head for a pillow. The jacket had once looked tailor-made sharp, but that was before he boarded the ancient bus. He caught sight of his reflection – hatless, coatless, tieless, and nearly shirtless – and figured that it didn't make all that much difference. He was still the returning hero. Maybe they'd have a big sign up to welcome him at the Danville depot.

The thought roused him from his stupor. Sitting up, he stretched his arms, popped a stick of Juicy Fruit into his mouth, and began to count the miles as he thought about his family and friends. They'd all be waiting for him, sign or no sign. His mother, his grandma Scott, his buddies Peewee and Leroy. He'd tell his mother and grandma that the Battle of the Bulge hadn't been so bad and that General Patton had been real nice – that was all they'd need to know. Or, at any rate, all they'd want to hear. And he'd tell Peewee and the gang about the real fighting, the German bullets whizzing overhead, and, best of all, about the sexy French girls who told him he looked like an African prince. 'Erotic' was what they'd called him.

The flavor was gone from the Juicy Fruit when the outskirts of Danville appeared, then the depot. The whole town seemed to have got smaller, especially the depot. The bus stopped, and Wendell did the best he could to straighten his uniform, then hauled down his duffel bag as the few white passengers got off. Now it was his turn. Goddamn, where *was* everyone?

He saw his mother and Grandma Scott as he descended the stairs of the bus. They were standing on tiptoe, craning their necks, and he couldn't make out if they were laughing or crying. He was home! Goddamn, he was really home, and he didn't know whether to laugh or cry himself!

'Wen-DELL! Over here!' His grandma came lumbering toward him, arms outstretched, and Wendell momentarily feared for his life. She was a big old woman, older than the hills – always had been, it seemed – and stronger than a lumberjack. Man, thought Wendell, she don't slow down, she's gonna knock me flat on my ass. She misjudge and run me over, I'm dead.

The old woman caught him in a bone-shattering embrace, but Wendell didn't mind the pain. He freed a hand and reached out to touch his mother's face. She was crying softly. Then it was her time to hug and kiss him.

'You okay, son' his mother asked, over and over, and Wendell, hugging and kissing and trying not to cry, nodded that he was. Not that he had the breath to answer, anyhow, what with all the squeezing and hugging. He had been away four long years, and it looked as if they were trying to make up for lost time all at once.

Grandma Scott finally disengaged herself to demand, 'Boy, you forget how to talk in that army?'

Wendell choked.

'Now, you hear me, boy. I said to you, you forget how to talk in that white man's army? You gonna answer your aged, most likely dying grandma, or do I take you over my knee and give your behind a good whacking?' The old woman let out a great whoop of laughter.

'Grandma,' said Wendell, 'you sure are tougher than any drill sergeant.' Grinning at his mother, he added, 'It sure is good to see both of you. You both look great, pretty as chorus girls. Grandma, you sure you wasn't ever in show business?'

'You just the same sweet-talking man you ever was,' Grandma Scott said, trying to look stern.

Wendell's mother continued to look him over and touch him gently. 'Son, it sure is good to see you,' she said. 'But it looks as if you lost a whole lot of weight. How they feed you in the army? I bet you never got nothing good – you'd better come home right now so we can start to fatten you up.'

As they left the station, Wendell felt a moment of disappointment. Nobody could be more important than his family, but where were his friends? Where were Peewee and the old crowd? Here he'd been busting his ass dodging bullets, up to his eyes in mud and snow, and there they'd been, living off the fat of the land, chasing every pretty girl in Virginia. Well, the hell with them!

Still, he had to ask. 'Grandma, Momma, how come nobody's here? I figured there'd be at least a brass band at the station, or at least that crowd of damn loafers I been defending for four years. Hell, I *am* a conquering hero.'

The two women spoke at once. 'Don't you say nobody's here . . . we here . . . your grandma and I've been waiting here for hours.'

'Conquering hero?' Grandma Scott added. 'Only thing you're gonna conquer is a tub of hot water. Look at you! And don't fret about your friends – they got their own lives, got their own things to do.'

Wendell forgot his annoyance to tease the old lady. 'Grandma, I think you've lived your whole life preaching the gospel according to a tub of hot water. Every day a baptism. Born again! Born again! Immerse me in water, Lord, I'm born again!' He slapped his knee and laughed.

'Don't blaspheme against the Lord,' his grandma said seriously. 'Now let's get out of here and start getting some meat on your bones. Hang around much longer and we'll miss the bus.'

'We're not going to miss no bus. We're going to take ourselves home in style,' announced Wendell, as he led the women toward old Pops Foster's beat-up cab. 'We are taking a taxi.'

'Taxi?' muttered Grandma Scott. 'They must have made you plumb crazy while you was in the army. Money don't grow on trees around here.'

'Grandma, I got lots of mustering-out pay. No more buses for me! Not ever – and especially not today. My bones still ache from sitting in that old rattletrap the whole way from Newport News. From now on, its strictly automobiles for me.'

'What do you mean, "from now on"?' Grandma Scott snorted. 'Automobiles all it's ever been your whole life. You just the same as your daddy, always crazy about speed. I remember how you'd race anything on your bike when you was a kid – Buicks, Packards, nothing was too big for you to take on. I was always sure that one day they'd bring you home all busted up in pieces. Same way I was sure they'd send you home from the army. Now that you home in one piece, boy, you just slow down awhile.'

'It's going to be automobiles! I been thinking about what to do now that I'm home. I may even buy my own taxi.' Wendell handed the women into the cab with a flourish.

II

The Scott house stood next to Grandma's grocery store, both small frame buildings like many others in the black section of Danville. Behind the house was the tool shed in which Wendell had spent countless hours messing with his bike, trying to get it to go faster. If the depot had looked smaller than Wendell's memory of it, the house and store looked smaller still.

He held the screen door open so the two women could precede him into the dark house. 'Okay, ladies, I'm ready for my hot bath,' he said.

All hell broke loose. When Mrs Scott turned on the light, the first thing he saw was the banner: WELCOME HOME WENDELL. Then the faces – about everyone he'd ever known in his whole life was here, aunts and uncles, nephews and nieces, bike-riding buddies, drag-racing buddies, every neighbor for it must be ten-twelve blocks. Old folks, young folks, even a few people Wendell couldn't remember ever having seen before. And all of them smiling and hugging and kissing, and everyone trying to talk at once, in a scene that suddenly made the Battle of the Bulge look pretty tame. Even if he'd been allowed to, Wendell couldn't have said a word.

He was half pushed, half carried to a huge trestle table covered to the edges with fried chicken, grits, spare ribs, potato salad, pecan pie, and everything else he'd dreamed about while freezing his ass off in Europe over a can of K rations. There was lemonade, sweet wine, and white lightning to wash down the food and, as the phonograph came alive, Coleman Hawkins and Benny Carter and Billie Holliday and Ella began to compete with the shouting in the room.

'You come back lookin' like a man,' said one neighbor,

grasping Wendell's hand. Another man slapped him on the back, calling him 'you old son of a gun,' and a chorus of voices from every direction demanded that he 'come on over here so we can get a look at you.' Wendell's head began to spin.

Suddenly one voice stood out above the others. 'That's Wendell Scott,' the voice said, 'General Patton's right-hand man.'

'That's got to be my main man,' said Wendell. He turned, eyes closed, like a magician performing a memory trick, his arms extended toward his friend. 'That's Peewee, unless the army made me a blind man and a fool.' He opened his eyes. 'Hey, Peewee!'

The two men embraced, grinning.

'Goddamn, Peewee, I don't know if I'd been able to recognize you if I'd had my eyes open. Four years ago you was small, but you must be shrinking. Man, you've gotten *shorter*.'

The little man giggled. 'Well, Wendell, I'd recognize you anywhere by your tall mouth. But what's a nice colored boy like you doing in a soldier suit?' The two friends slapped palms, laughing.

Wendell took off his Eisenhower jacket, tossed it on a chair, and returned to the attack. 'Look at yourself. Where'd you get them fancy clothes? Damn, but you look like one fancy dude in that zoot suit. Course the suit is bigger than you are, but that don't make no difference because pretty much everything's bigger than you are. You turning into a pretty boy, Peewee?'

Peewee turned to Wendell's mother in mock indignation. 'Mrs Scott, get your boy out of here. He don't show the proper respect for us gentlemen of leisure.' He brushed some imaginary lint from his padded shoulders, adjusted the extra-wide knot of his extra-wide tie, then snapped his fingers under Wendell's nose. 'Pretty boy or not, Wendell, I got women falling all over me.'

'Falling, hell, they *tripping* over you,' Wendell managed to get in before he was carried off on another round of 'Good to see you's.'

A few minutes later, Peewee was back at his side, pressing a glass of clear liquid into his hand. 'You never tasted anything like this,' Peewee said, as Wendell took a long exploratory swig. 'This stuff's the best. I get it straight from the best still in the hills. This is the real moonshine, my friend, and it'll put hair on your teeth.'

The speech was rudely interrupted; Wendell's knees had buckled. Groping blindly for a glass of ice water, he managed to gasp out a few words. 'Goddamn,' he choked. 'You call that the best? Jesus, I hope I never get to taste the worst!' He recovered his voice, although his guts were still full of fire. 'You sure that ain't rubbing alcohol?'

The party was warming up. Leroy Wiggins, another old buddy, was performing his imitation of Satchel Paige, food and drink were being passed and consumed, and couples had begun to dance. As Leroy finished his impersonation, flat on the floor, a young girl walked straight up to Wendell. 'I want to dance with a real live hero,' she said. Wendell didn't recognize her, but he wasn't about to complain. Twenty-one or twenty-two, he thought, and a real looker. And about as full of mischief as some of those French girls.

'I'm no hero,' Wendell said, wondering if he should be so honest.

'Well, anyhow, you're a live one, aincha, soldier boy?' the girl teased.

'No soldier boy, either, not any more. Who are you anyway?'

'I'm Sissy Carter. You and me went to school together, except I was the quiet little girl who sat way at the back of the class. Your friend Peewee said it was okay for me to come tonight. Is it okay?'

'Sure is, but how come I don't remember you?'

'Because I was just a little girl, and you were out drag-racing and busting heads and having a good time with your friends, and never looked at me.' She spoke demurely enough, but her eyes never stopped flirting.

Wendell grabbed her and moved with her into a slow fox-trot. 'Well,' he said, 'you sure did a lot of growing up while I was gone. In fact, it looks to me like you're about ready to move up to the head of the class.'

'Weeeooo! Lock up your daughters! Wendell is home from the wars!' shouted Peewee, pausing in flight, happy that his friend was home.

Wendell held Sissy tightly as they moved to the music.

Her, or the noise and the smoke, or simply seeing so many people he loved in the same place at the same time – whatever it was, he was beginning to feel dizzy. Excusing himself, he removed his tie and loosened his collar. 'You feeling all right?' Sissy asked solicitously. She went across the room and returned with a tumbler of moonshine. 'You want a little sip of this, help you settle down?'

'No, thanks,' said Wendell. 'I'm fine, just fine. I'm just not used to all the noise and excitement after the peace and quiet of World War II. I think I'll just take a little fresh air. But don't you go away, because I'll be right back, and when I come back, Miss Sissy Carter, I am personally going to crown you Queen of the Wendell Scott Homecoming Ball.'

Sissy nodded happily as he quickly crossed the room and went out the back door.

Wendell needed time to breathe, to think. Almost automatically, he crossed the yard and entered the tool shed. When he turned on the light, he was once again in the midst of his childhood dreams – the pictures of automobiles and automobile racers tacked to the walls of the musty shed, in the corner the bike upon which he had run so many races between stints of delivering groceries for his grandma's store.

He was deep in thought when the old lady entered the shed. 'What you doing in here by yourself,' she demanded. 'Don't you know, *you* the guest of honor! You feeling all right?'

'Just wanted to get myself together,' Wendell answered softly. 'Decide what to do for myself. I been thinking about that all the time I was away. Like I told you, I think I'll get me a car and start a taxi service – old Pops Foster ain't going to offer much competition. And then maybe I'll save up my money and buy a service station, too.'

'That all sounds real good, honey,' his grandma said encouragingly.

He looked about twelve years old again, she thought, with that wild-assed gleam in his eye that she remembered well.

Without warning, Wendell lifted the big old woman off the ground and twirled her around. 'And then,' he laughed, panting under her weight, 'then, I'm going to get me the fastest damn car you ever saw, and I'm going to race it all over the damn country, and I'm going to win all my damn races and be a big national hero, just like Wilbur Shaw.'

'Put me down, boy, and watch your mouth,' said Grandma Scott. But she was smiling as Wendell set her gently down.

'What you going to do then, Mr National Hero?' she asked.

'Well, hell, Grandma, when I get tired of winning all those races, I guess I'll become President of the United States. What else will be left?'

Arm in arm, they returned to the laughter and noise of the party.

III

Two days after his return home, Wendell bought himself his taxi. At first the used car dealers in Danville tried to unload every old dog they had on him, the worst traps on the premises, but then they got a look at his roll and fell all over themselves showing him something 'more suitable' for that great wad of mustering-out money.

Wendell's expertise helped him choose a good 1939 Lincoln Zephyr. Not for nothing had he put in four years overhauling and maintaining army rolling stock, from Jeeps to Sherman tanks. His mechanical aptitude had always been great, and from messing around with his bike as a kid he had progressed to master mechanic. There was really no kind of machine with which Wendell couldn't mess around; by the time he was through, that machine would be as good as new and, with any luck, twice as fast. It drove the used-car dealers crazy, the way he tore apart their stock before their very eyes. He drove home in the '39 Zephyr pleased with himself and the car.

The following day he took the Zephyr over to Jenkins's sign shop and watched with pride as Jenkins lettered the words 'Scott's Taxi Service' on each side. Damn, but those words did look pretty! His next stop was at city hall, where he signed a number of papers with his full name – Wendell Oliver Scott – and paid the requisite fees. A lot of paperwork was involved, but Wendell was finally in business.

Business, he soon discovered, wasn't all that good. Even the white cabs were hurting for passengers. A lot of his time seemed to be spent just hanging around the bus depot, waiting for the fares and shooting the shit with one or two of the other drivers. Mostly the black folks just got off one bus, then lined up for seats at the back of another one.

'Whew! This is one tough way to make a buck,' said Pops Foster.

'All ways to make a buck is tough,' said Wendell. 'Now, come on, Pops. Let's get a smile going on that face of yours. Times are changing. Why, some day, man, you going to actually see the white folk riding in our taxis.'

'I ain't never going to live to see that day,' said Pops. 'Hell, white folk ride in our cabs, they afraid the color might rub off on them.' He let out a short laugh.

'And,' Wendell continued, 'our people going to be so prosperous, they going to be riding in white cabs.'

'Shit, no, man,' said Pops. 'They going to have limousines.' They both doubled up on that one.

The real hell of driving a taxi, though, was that with traffic and speed limits, and passengers always wanting to stop for some damn thing, Wendell couldn't work up any speed. Once in a while, he'd give himself a little vacation – go out in the country, let the Zephyr go full throttle and scare the hell out of the cows. But it wasn't enough.

One day Wendell let it all run away with him. He was sitting in his cab, parked a few feet down the block from the Maples Hotel, finishing off the sandwiches and coffee that his mother had packed for him, when he spotted a fare. Not that spotting him required good eyesight – the man, clearly a drummer, must have weighed three hundred pounds. He was coming out of the hotel, followed by Willard, the Maples's skinny old porter, who was toting the man's bulging valise and stuffed sample case.

Wendell started the cab and was at the door of the hotel before the man had even begun to signal. Nonetheless, the fat man waved imperiously at Wendell with his tightly rolled umbrella. This one's going to be a pain in the ass, thought Wendell, but he's a real live passenger.

'Taxi, mister?' he asked pleasantly.

The fat man nodded. Wendell stopped the cab and got out to inquire, 'Put those suitcases in the luggage compartment, sir?'

'Don't you bother,' said the fat salesman. 'I know your tricks – charging extra for the luggage compartment and all that. I'm going to put my things right in the back with me.'

While Willard struggled to fit the cases in the back seat

of the cab, Wendell studied the fat man. He had never seen fat like this. This had to be the fattest ever – this dude was so fat that his head looked about the size of a peanut. Well-dressed though, must be doing well. Sharp, three-piece black pinstripe suit, black homburg hat, and that goddamn little umbrella. Probably put his own eye out with it sometime, way he's waving it around.

Snickering to himself at the last thought, Wendell got back in the driver's seat and adjusted his cap at a jaunty angle. Fats was now harassing Willard, telling him he hadn't got all day.

As Willard backed out of the cab, the drummer reached into his vest pocket and withdrew a dime. Willard accepted the princely tip, muttering, and when the fat man had squeezed in beside his luggage, he slammed the cab door hard.

If old Willard been any faster, Wendell thought, he might have got himself about a five-pound slice of lard. 'Where to, sir?' he asked.

'I'm going to the station, and make sure you take the direct route,' Fats said. 'I know all about the tricks you people play on out-of-towners, and you might as well know right now that I'm not going to sit still for any of them.'

'Yes, boss,' Wendell dead-panned. Oh shit! he thought. He shifted fast from first into second, and watched the salesman's knees shoot up toward the roof as the cab lurched.

'Can't you be more careful?' said the drummer.

'Yes, boss,' said Wendell.

Teach him a little something, he thought as he set off toward the station. He knew the city like the back of his hand; knew to the second, when the lights would change, where the traffic would be heavy or light, and all the best shortcuts. He'd get his fussy fare to the station on time, and then some.

A police siren sounded behind him, and he pulled to the side. A green Dodge shot past, going faster than greased lightning and Wendell recognized the soul-satisfying sound of a souped-up engine. Then the pursuing patrol car went by, damn near as fast. Wendell's fat passenger was also watching the chase with interest.

'See that?' said Wendell. 'That man was really hauling ass. Got to be a liquor runner.'

'Damn bootleggers are a disgrace to the whole race,' the salesman said.

God, thought Wendell, I suppose this cheap bastard thinks he's an ornament to it! He slammed the cab's accelerator to the floor. The Lincoln had a hopped-up mill of its own, and just for the pure joy of it, he set out after the patrol car.

For a few seconds his passenger did not realize what was happening, and he continued to babble about the immorality of bootleggers, and how they don't care about what the white community thinks, and how we Negroes have to think about our image and our self-respect. Then he was struck blessedly speechless with the knowledge that he was probably going to be killed by this madman whom he had mistaken for a God-fearing taxi driver.

'Stop this very instant!' the fat man gasped. 'Are you crazy? I want to get to the station. Are you insane? This isn't the way to the station. *Let me out of here!*' His eyes were bulging with fright and rage.

Wendell had better things to think about. 'Quit yammering and hang on,' he said. 'I'll get you to the god-damn station in goddamn good time.'

The cab was now directly behind the patrol car, following it in and out of side streets, past screeching, braking trucks and open-mouthed pedestrians. Then the three speeding cars were beyond the city limits, heading for the country. The green sedan was doing ninety, the patrol car was hanging in at about the same speed, and Wendell was riding their slipstream, comfortable as could be. Slower-moving traffic posed no problem – at the sound of the siren, the few cars and trucks ahead would slow down and pull over. After one look at the passing parade, they sheared clean off the road.

Wendell began to hum. He was happier than hell, and completely oblivious to the unfortunate passenger in the back seat.

The fat man had begun to consider that he might be being kidnapped. 'How much money do you want,' he pleaded. 'I'll give you double the fare if you'll only turn around. And I won't say a word to anyone. Honest.

Please! I'm a family man. Here, look, there are my wife and children! Two little girls. I'm their sole support. Don't kill me! You can have my sample cases, anything. You just name it. But *stop*, please, for the sweet Lord's sake!'

Wendell couldn't ignore him any more; the babbling had become distracting. 'I don't want your money,' he said in his most reassuring tone, 'and I don't want your life history, and I don't want your damn old sample cases. You just relax and enjoy the view. I'll get you to the station on time, just like I said I would. Now you just take it nice and easy – and *relax*!'

As he spoke the last word, the patrol car ahead missed a turn and bounced crazily off into a field.

'Can we quit now?' asked the fat man feebly.

'Goddamn it, relax!' said Wendell. 'I got me some business to do.'

The Lincoln drew up alongside the Dodge. Wendell looked steadily at the driver, and the driver looked at him. Wendell knew who the other man was – Henry Simms, one of the meanest men in the bootlegging trade. Both cars slowed, so that conversation was possible as they moved along side by side.

'Hey, man, you crazy,' said Simms. 'Who the hell are you anyhow? You like to get killed, and for what notion?'

'Scott. Wendell Scott. I drive a cab. That back there's my passenger.'

The fat drummer saw another chance to reason with Wendell. 'Please,' he whimpered, 'if you just take me to the station, I won't say nothing.' He was silenced by simultaneous glares – impatient from Wendell, just plain fearsome from the bootlegger.

'No shit,' said Simms to Wendell. 'Now get off my ass.'

'Listen,' said Wendell, 'I want me some action, and you might be just the man to provide some.'

Clearly this cat was crazy, Simms thought. But he might be useful. 'Okay, Wendell Scott,' he replied, 'you tell me what you want, 'cause I got better things to do than chat all afternoon.'

'Look,' said Wendell, 'I can drive fast, and I can make a car run. Ain't nobody better than me. You want that, I'm your man.'

'Ever haul liquor?'

It was the question Wendell had expected. 'Nope. But I can handle it. I know every back road, front road, side road, and cow path in this county.' And I've damned well shown you how I can drive, he thought.

'Okay, then,' said Simms. 'You get Uncle Tom there to the station before he turns any whiter, and you meet me tonight at Sweets'. About ten o'clock. Got it?'

'Damn right I got it,' said Wendell.

Simms accelerated and moved on up the road, while Wendell pulled off a sharp U-turn and headed back to town. Hot damn! he was thinking – a little moonshine, a lot of money.

He took the direct route to the station and delivered what was left of his passenger with a minute or two to spare. He was so elated that he forgot to collect his fare.

IV

Sweets' was where you went for just about anything. Something to drink, something to smoke, something to sniff. A little gambling. A few girls. Or a place to pass the time talking business or baseball. The neon sign in the saloon's single window was more often off than on, but it didn't matter much. Folks knew how to find Sweets', whether it advertised itself or not, and the parking lot was always filled with cars, from big Caddies to beat-up Fords and Chevvies. Family men frequented Sweets' when they wanted a night on the town, but they sure as hell didn't bring their wives. The women on the premises were both useful and decorative.

Wendell hadn't been in the club for five years. That time, Peewee and he, as spruced up as they could be, had swaggered in set to howl. They had been asked for their identification by a giggling barmaid (for whom Peewee had already formed some plans) and had been denied service. They swaggered right out again, Wendell feeling sheepish, Peewee set for a brawl.

Wendell laughed to himself at the recollection. Goddamn, even then Peewee had been ready to take on just about anyone. Tonight was different, though. Tonight he didn't need any I.D. And tonight was going to be all business.

The noise and the smoke hit him spang in the face as he opened the door at exactly ten o'clock. Goddamn if it didn't look like New Year's Eve, he thought. He flattened himself out against the wall to the left of the long, busy bar, and surveyed the room. The dance floor, a space the size of a handkerchief, was crowded with couples, glued together with sweat and showing no particular interest in keeping time with the music. The women, regulars of the place, mostly wore bras shaped like ice-cream cones, net stockings, and more makeup than French whores. Even from where he stood, Wendell could smell their perfume above the smoke. Traffic streamed around him – a large number of men with silk shirts and big pinky rings seemed to be making entrances and exits. Or maybe it was all the same man and he was just very damn busy. One part of Wendell was enjoying the scene, the other wanted to run. He reminded himself that even if he felt like a wet-behind-the-ears country boy, he was still the fastest driver in Danville, and everyone else would soon know it.

He jumped as a hand touched his arm. Hot damn! he thought. Been here one minute, and already some girl's after me.

The hand, however, belonged to Simms. 'Welcome to Sweets',' said the bootlegger. 'You right on time.' He led Wendell to an empty table and beckoned a waitress.

'Two more over here, honey,' he said.

'Two more what?' asked Wendell.

'I'm drinking gin. That okay with you?' Simms inquired, making it sound like a threat.

'Little taste of gin's fine with me,' Wendell said, thinking that he couldn't afford to let this bad-assed cat get him too drunk to transact serious business. The waitress scurried back with two jiggers of gin and a couple of ginger-ale set-ups. She gave Wendell an appraising look that made him blush.

Simms sipped his drink. 'Scott,' he said, 'I've been doing some checking around on you, and you seem to be okay. You got any kind of record? Ever had any trouble with the law at all? Not just here in Danville, but anywhere, ever?'

Keep cool, Wendell reminded himself, just keep cool. 'In answer to your question did I ever have any trouble with the law, I –'

'Goddamn it, Scott,' said Simms. 'I *know* what the goddamn question was. Now just give me a straight yes or no answer.'

'No,' said Wendell.

'And you want to make some money driving – well, we won't talk about what.'

'How much money do you think I can pull?' asked Wendell eagerly.

Simms laughed and slapped down his hands with such force that the whole table shook. Still laughing, he snapped his fingers at the waitress for another round. 'That's what I like about you, boy,' he said in a comfortable voice that scared the hell out of Wendell. 'Straight to the point. Okay. I'd say you're good for forty, fifty, a night. And that's just the beginning.'

As Simms leaned forward with the air of a banker closing a loan, Wendell saw the marks along his throat and cheek. Shit, he thought, either this dude is just as mean as he looks, or else he sure is clumsy shaving.

'But you know,' Simms went on, 'that if the Man gets you, there isn't anything at all that I'm going to do for you. You on your own. And you never talk about nothing to no one. You get caught, stay deaf and dumb – you talk, you're dead. You cross me once, and that's the only time you live to cross anybody. Got it?'

Wendell had it. 'When do I start?'

'Man, you already started,' said Simms, extending his hand. 'You got a car?'

'Yeah,' said Wendell. 'I picked me up a trap today. It's over by Leffert's place. Old Hudson. I been working on it most of the afternoon.'

'You move fast, boy, and I like that,' Simms said. 'Now you be over at the white graveyard up north of town at two o'clock this morning. You just park and sit real quiet, and someone will come and take you up in the hills.'

As Wendell began to repeat these instructions, one of Sweets' more spectacular girls passed the table and gave him the eye. Watching her tall, tantalizing figure, Wendell let out a long, low whistle. 'Why don't you send her?' he asked Simms. 'She can take me up in the hills any old time.'

Simms motioned the girl toward their table. She seemed to hesitate, but changed her mind pretty fast when Simms rose and sauntered toward her. Uh-oh, Wendell thought, I don't want to owe no favors to Henry Simms, and this chick doesn't look too eager to give any out.

Simms came back to the table, smiling big, the girl following him.

'You got eyes, Scott?' he said. 'Well, you're in luck, because this young lady's got real big eyes for young bootleggers.'

Wendell realized that his whistle had been bravado. He was plain damn scared of this girl, just as he was plain damn scared of Simms.

'What you talking about?' he asked Simms, playing the country boy.

'For someone so fast, you sure are slow, boy. You got yourself a lady,' Simms said, indicating the girl with a flick of his hand. 'That's my way of welcoming you to the club.'

'I surely do appreciate your gesture, Simms,' Wendell replied, then added, 'but I think I see an old friend sitting over there all by her lonesome, and I really should pay my respects.' He waved to a girl across the room. Thank the Lord, she waved back. Simms squinted through the smoke at her.

'Very nice, Mr Scott. But she don't look so old to me. And say, how come I never seen you around here before? You sure you a local boy?'

'I been away, Mr Simms, away in this man's army. That's one reason you don't have to worry about me talking. Name, rank, and serial number only!' Wendell laughed, stood up to slap palms with Simms, and set out through the noise and smoke toward the girl across the room.

The girl wasn't as young as she'd looked through the haze, but her smile, when Wendell sat down at her table, had a glint of genuine shyness to it. He began to wonder if maybe she wasn't an old friend. Sissy Carter, after all, had come as a big surprise. You never could tell how little girls were going to grow up.

'Do I know you?' he asked.

'You waved at me,' the girl said.

'Yeah,' Wendell admitted, 'but I didn't expect you to wave back.'

'Well, don't be so down in the mouth about it, sugar,' she said. 'You could hurt a lady's feelings.' Her smile had become a hell of a lot less shy. She finished her drink, grabbed Wendell's leg under the table, and said almost briskly, 'Where we going, lover?'

Goddamn, thought Wendell, things are sure happening fast tonight. 'Some place quiet,' he said.

'Sounds good,' said the girl. 'Is it far?'

Some place quiet so he could think about tonight's liquor run, was what Wendell really had in mind. He needed to be alone and to concentrate, but he most definitely did not want to hurt this lady's feelings. Inspiration seized him. 'It's not too far,' he said, 'but we'll take a cab, anyhow.'

'A cab? Ooooh!' she squealed. 'Oh, you and me's going to get along just fine!'

The girl got up and swayed toward the entrance. Dropping a couple of bills on the table, Wendell followed her, aware that Simms's eyes were on him.

They crossed the parking lot, and the girl's eyes lit up when she saw the big Lincoln. Casually, Wendell opened the back door for her. She got in and stretched out her long, full legs, revolving her left foot slightly to show off the ankle. She leaned back on the seat, and turned to Wendell with a big smile. She looked surprised as hell when he closed the door on her and got into the driver's seat.

'Now you just tell me what in the name of sweet Jesus is going on here,' she demanded. 'You some kind of a pervert?'

'I told you we were going in a taxi,' Wendell said. He turned on the dome light and adjusted his driver's cap at a rakish angle so that she could get a better look at its legend, 'Scott's Taxi Service'.

'Where to, miss?' he asked politely.

The girl was laughing so hard that two or three times Wendell thought she might fall right out on the street. In fact, she thought it was all so damned funny that Wendell had little trouble persuading her to let him drop her off at a corner of her choice.

V

It was cold in the graveyard, colder than the damp, chill autumn air and the early hour could fully account for. Wendell shivered. He sure didn't believe in spooks, but at a quarter of two in the morning, following a day that had seen him transformed into a bootlegger and a ladies' man, he didn't know quite what he did believe. He jumped three feet in the air when an owl hooted, then managed a nervous giggle.

He tried to keep warm by jogging among the tombstones, but jogging made too much noise on the gravel paths. He tried to amuse himself by reading the inscriptions, but the cold brought tears to his eyes, and even by the bright light of the moon, the stones remained mostly indecipherable. Probably wouldn't have been much fun, anyway, Wendell thought. He wished he'd brought a sweater. He rubbed his hands together, fighting the chill. He wished he'd brought gloves. Or an oil stove, or any damn thing, just to be warm. He wished he'd brought the girl, for that matter. No matter what Simms said about coming alone, he'd be a lot happier right now with a little company.

And Jesus Christ! He *had* company! A clammy hand touched the back of his neck, and Wendell fought back a scream. He turned slowly. When he saw Peewee standing there, cool and composed, he didn't know what to think. Was this a practical joke? What the hell was *Peewee*, of all the people on God's green earth, doing in the white cemetery at two o'clock in the morning?

Peewee tipped his wide-brimmed hat. 'Evening, Scott,' he said casually.

'"Evening, Scott", my ass,' said Wendell. 'Peewee, what the hell you doing creeping round here like some goddamn vampire, scaring the shit out of God-fearing folk?'

Peewee ostentatiously brushed some dirt off his blue suede shoes. 'It seems to me,' he said, 'that I might ask just what the hell *you* doing here, Mr Wendell Oliver Scott?'

Wendell remembered his mission. He looked around to make sure that no one was within earshot. 'I got an important business meeting,' he said. 'And I'm dealing with some pretty rough customers who aren't going to like it if they see I got company. So I suggest that whatever you up to, you get that little black ass of yours out of here damn fast. I say this for your own good, my man.'

'No shit?' said Peewee.

Oh, God, thought Wendell, why did he have to have such dumb friends? The little man might really be in danger. 'Look, boy, like I said, get out of here! Now. I got a no-shit important business meeting about any minute.'

'You bet your sweet ass you got an important business meeting, Wendell Scott,' drawled Peewee. His casualness was maddening. 'And you at the right place, the right time, with the right man. You got an important business meeting with *me*, nigger. You ain't the only one around here that knows Mr Henry Simms.'

Wendell shook his head. 'Well, I'll be damned,' he said. 'If that don't beat all.' But suddenly it all made sense. Of course! Any party, it was Peewee that brought the moonshine. There were the threads and the women and the money. And the cigars, the expensive ones, like the one Peewee was now offering him.

'Well, I *will* be damned!' Wendell repeated, as he took the cigar and accepted a light. He looked at his friend with new respect.

For a while, the two of them just stood there, smoking the fine Havana tobacco. Then, suddenly, Peewee let out a whoop. 'Hey, partner!' he yelled.

'Hey, partner, yourself!' Wendell yelled right back, and they were still laughing as they moved toward Wendell's moonshining car, the old Hudson he had bought and fixed up earlier that day. The engine purred smoothly when he turned the key in the ignition. He had made a pretty good afternoon's work of it. The body still looked like hell, but the motor worked just fine.

The hilly roads back of the cemetery were new territory for Wendell, despite his earlier boast to Simms. Hell, some of them weren't even cowpaths! Peewee guided him, directing him when to cut the lights. The still they were going to visit tonight wasn't the only one hereabouts, and passing strangers had to be cautious. Moonshiners around here were likely to take a shot at an unfamiliar car, since any unidentifiable automobile might be filled with Federal revenue officers. Shoot first, ask later, had always proved to be an effective rule when carrying on an illegal trade. Even when Wendell was allowed to use his lights, there was nothing to see except tall, grim trees beside the climbing dirt road.

Peewee directed him off a sorry dirt road onto an even sorrier one and then told him suddenly to douse the lights. The little man's whisper was urgent. 'Just take it slow and easy now, you hear, Wendell? There, now, see them boards across that ditch? Just drive up over those, then I'll get out and pull them across after us, and that way the law can't find no tracks. Pretty sharp arrangement, ain't it?' He giggled.

Wendell eased across the embankment, then stopped while Peewee went back for the boards. His mind was racing. He'd been up since seven o'clock the preceding morning, and it had been a damned busy day, but he felt fully awake. More than awake. He was facing a new challenge, and he might not come out of it with a whole hide.

Peewee got back in the Hudson and they drove on slowly. A few feet from the ditch, Wendell made out the silhouette of a man with a shotgun. A moment later, they emerged in a clearing in the woods. On the far side of the clearing was a small wooden shack.

'Cut your motor,' said Peewee. 'We're here.'

Acting on a sudden hunch, Wendell made a sharp U-turn, pointing the Hudson back down the track.

'Why you do that?' asked Peewee.

'Just a feeling I got,' said Wendell.

When they emerged from the car, they were instantly surrounded by a group of heavily armed white men.

Wendell couldn't quite make out how many of them there were, but it sure as hell wasn't any rabbit-hunting party. In total silence, Peewee and he were escorted to the shack. Wendell had no intention of trying to start any social conversation, anyhow. Gang like this, a simple 'Good evening' could get a man a bellyful of buckshot. Blast you as soon as pick the tobacco out of their teeth.

One of the white men pushed open the door of the shack. The interior was lighted by kerosene lamps and crammed with cases of moonshine, from dirt floor to sagging ceiling. There was hardly room to stand. Wendell could see now that there were five of the white men, all mean-looking bastards. Still no one spoke. The white men looked at Wendell, and Wendell looked at the cases of white lightning, hoping to God that no one struck a match. The kerosene lamps made him nervous enough. At last a back door opened, and a big, bearded man came in, accompanied by a small, red-haired fellow, who nodded to Peewee. It was only the slightest sign of civility, but it made Wendell feel better. He'd begun to wonder if this was a lynching party, rather than an important business meeting.

'Who's he?' the bearded man asked Peewee, indicating Wendell.

'New driver for Simms,' Peewee answered. 'Name's Wendell Scott.'

And then Peewee began making introductions all around. 'This here's the owner of this operation,' he said to Wendell, nodding at the big mountain man, 'and these others, except the one with red hair, are his sons who help him in the business.' Looking around the circle of mean-eyed, blank faces, Wendell wondered if any of them had ever smiled. Even when they were little babies. Probably not, with a daddy like that.

The red-haired man was introduced as a fellow bootlegger, the one who ran the stuff to the old man's white clientele. Peewee didn't mention his name.

The distiller looked at Wendell. 'I guarantee you be safe anywhere in this county, boy,' he said solemnly.

'He's got the police in his back pocket,' said Peewee, clearly trying to suck up to the boss.

'But boy, once you cross that county line, you on your own,' the bearded man cautioned.

'Shit,' said Wendell, tiring of the tone of the interview, 'the county line's only three miles away.'

'I'd watch my mouth if I was you, boy,' the old man said. 'And the rest of you better stop jawing and start loading.'

Peewee joined the old man and his sons in forming a line between the shack and the Hudson. Silently, the men passed the cases of moonshine from hand to hand, loading them into the trunk and back seat of Wendell's car.

Wendell approached the white bootlegger's car. The red-haired man was leaning against it, whistling softly. 'Want a look?' he asked. 'Name's Jackson, by the way. Albert Jackson.'

The car was a red-and-black Mercury sedan. Jackson produced a flashlight from his hip pocket, then opened the right front and rear doors so that Wendell could inspect the interior. There was just one seat in the big car, directly behind the wheel. The rest of the interior was empty. 'More room for the moon,' Jackson explained. 'Now let me show you something else.'

He played the light on the floor next to the driver's seat. There were two gearshifts, and Wendell studied them with interest.

'Betcha never seen nothing like that before, have you, boy?' Jackson did not wait for an answer. 'You sure as hell haven't. Little invention of my own. This old Merc's got two transmissions. That's right, two! One for going forward, one for reverse. Now, I don't have to be backing into no narrow streets. Beats throwing a fast U, if you got steady hands and iron kidneys.'

Wendell gave a soft whistle of appreciation. Goddamn, that *was* something else! 'That's a real pretty piece of work,' he said. 'Like to have a closer look at that someday.'

'Well, you come 'round any time you want, boy. Like I said, the name's Albert Jackson, and I got me a garage on the south side of Danville. You just come any time.'

Peewee appeared out of the darkness in his shirtsleeves and sweating heavily. Wendell had never seen his friend look anything less than dapper, and the vision of this new Peewee – the one that might work with his hands – was as startling as the earlier apparition of Peewee the bootlegger. It had been an evening full of surprises.

'We all set to go,' Peewee said. 'Let's load this one up. Never know when we might want to get out of here right quick.'

Wendell joined the line, passing the cases of liquor to fill up Jackson's customized Mercury. The moon went behind the clouds, and it got so dark that he couldn't see the face of the man next to him. The procedure was simple. Wendell would move a few steps toward the shack to collect a case of moonshine, then move a few steps forward to pass the case on to Jackson, who loaded it in the car. Wendell did it several times, and then something seemed to be getting funny. Damned if the line didn't seem to be getting shorter, behind and before him. A few more passes, and he didn't have to move; he just stood still on the line as the cases of liquor were passed from hand to hand. Either that shack's got closer, he thought, or there are a lot more people here than there ought to be!

Wendell squinted through the darkness at the man next to him. Couldn't see much, but this dude looked like he'd shaved recently, or at any rate more recently than the moonshiner and his sons, and – by damn! – his denim work clothes smelled new. It didn't take a deep thinker to figure out what was happening.

Wendell waited until the man beside him had a case of liquor in his hands, and then shouted, 'The law! Run for it!'

He took his own advice and dashed for the Hudson as all hell broke out. Peewee was beside him in a second. From behind them came the sound of hand-to-hand combat, but Wendell didn't choose to stick around to see it. Besides, in the darkness, he couldn't tell his friends from his enemies. Let them take care of each other, he thought, and started the car.

VI

Gunfire rang out as the Hudson shot down the dirt track. Peewee tried to decide whether to jump in the back seat to protect the cargo of moonshine or just scrunch way down in the front seat to protect himself. He chose the latter. The way Wendell was driving, a man couldn't get too much protection.

'Slow down, man,' Peewee screamed, 'we coming to the ditch!'

Wendell slowed down, but not much. Thank God the planks were in place! Maybe the Man was planning on making a quick getaway himself. They bounced on, weaving crazily from side to side.

'You want to get us killed?' Peewee pleaded. 'You don't even know these roads, Wendell, you only been on them once, and then it was pitch black. You going to wrap us around a tree, man! And I'm too young to die – I got a good long life ahead of me, and you trying to make it short!'

The sound of gunfire faded, and Wendell began to enjoy himself. He was a real, no-shit bootlegger now, he thought, and the fastest thing on wheels. He was even beginning to enjoy Peewee's complaints.

'I plan to make me a lot of money and retire young,' Peewee babbled on. 'And I don't want no maniac driver spoiling those plans. You hear me, Wendell? You hear me, man? Please slow down. Please!' He tried to read the speedometer, but the needle was shooting back and forth so fast as the car swerved from side to side that he couldn't make it out. But they were sure going fast!

Wendell was now having himself a fine old time. He speeded up, though the turns were coming faster and sharper. 'C'mon, Peewee, stop fretting,' he said. 'I been on these roads once, that's all I need.' His voice was calm, as if he were just taking his grandma out for a Sunday drive, as the car ran down into a ditch on one side of the road and right back up again. Peewee slumped clear down on the floor and lay curled up under the dashboard. He seemed to be praying.

Wendell slowed down a little as they reached familiar farm country, and Peewee reappeared from under the dashboard, looking relieved. 'Where was you, man?' said Wendell. 'I thought you might have got yourself locked up in the glove compartment.'

Peewee did not rise to the bait about his size. 'It's a miracle,' he said solemnly, 'that we got out of there alive.'

'No miracle,' smiled Wendell. 'You riding with the best.'

And goddamn, he thought, if this old heap of a Hudson wasn't responding to his every wish. Almost seemed to drive itself, just running along through farm country. And it was a *fast* son of a bitch – he'd seen to that. He thought about taking it straight on down to the Danville Speedway, painting a big number on its side – he'd almost been partial to thirty-four – and racing the hell out of it. But first he'd better attend to business.

'That was only the beginning, up there in the hills,' Peewee said. 'We got away with our skins and a whole load, but now we got to deliver.'

'What the hell happened up there in the hills?' Wendell inquired. 'I thought that old coot was supposed to have all the police in his back pocket, so how come they come out shooting?'

'Those weren't the locals,' Peewee explained. 'Couldn't have been. That old coot really does own the county. But those were Federal men from Washington, D.C., and he don't own them. And we out of his county now, so we got to watch out for everyone.'

The farmhouses and barns whizzed by them, barely visible in the first hint of the dawn.

'Okay, friend,' said Peewee, 'now you put your dimmers on and drive real slow. I mean *real* slow, cause we don't want to make no noise. Turn into that next road up yonder.'

'Where we going?' asked Wendell.

'This here land's Mayor DuPree's farm,' said Peewee.

'Mayor DuPree?' asked Wendell in surprise, as he cut the Hudson's lights and drifted up the road. 'God Almighty, the mayor's a bootlegger, too?'

'Wouldn't surprise me none,' said Peewee. 'Anyhow, this is where we drop the stuff every Wednesday. I got me some of the farmhands on the payroll, and they look after things.'

At Peewee's direction, Wendell eased the Hudson off the road and parked alongside a barbed-wire fence posted with a 'No Trespassing' sign. A haystack stood about twenty feet away. The two men got out of the car, and as Peewee moved toward the fence, Wendell ran his hands carefully over the Hudson's fenders. Good! The Feds hadn't even made a dent in him!

Five minutes went by. Then two men appeared from behind the haystack, nodded to Peewee, and eyed Wendell with suspicion. 'Friend of mine,' explained Peewee. 'He'll be making the drops from now on.'

They all got down to business unloading the Hudson, and before long the moonshine was stashed safely away within the haystack. Peewee paid the men off with a thick wad of bills, and they vanished as silently as they had come.

Wendell looked at his friend, impressed once again, as they got back in the Hudson. Old Peewee's sure full of surprises, he thought.

Another surprise lay in store. Lights hit them before he had time to turn the key in the ignition. 'Goddamn if it ain't the law again!' muttered Peewee, lunging for the door. 'Shit, shit, *shit!*'

Wendell grabbed the little man and hugged him, pulling him down.

'Wendell, you gone crazy?' Peewee sputtered, struggling. 'That's the *law*, man!'

'You just stay real cool, and don't say nothing,' Wendell commanded. 'Just stay right here, and cuddle up real close. Goddamn it, I said *cuddle*! Otherwise I'll break your fool neck.'

Peewee couldn't have said a word if he'd wanted to.

'Now hear me good,' Wendell went on as the patrol car drew closer. 'We beat the Man once tonight, and we can do it again, if we just keep our heads. No point in running – can't beat a bullet and can't hide in a haystack full of moonshine. So you just snuggle up here and pretend like you my girl-friend. Relax and think pretty, and I'll cover up your tiny little head with my big loving hands. Got it?' He drew Peewee closer, blocking his vision and stifling his objections.

The Danville police cruiser stopped beside them, but the two cops did not get out. They were bored and tired, and their legs were stiff, and now, just when it looked like they were going to get some action – some moonshiners, maybe – all they had was a couple necking in a parked car. With all their clothes on, too. Shit! But maybe they could still have a little fun before the night was over.

'Hey,' said one of the cops, a burly blond, 'you see that bitch jump when the lights hit her?'

His partner, young and covered with pimples, snickered in reply.

'Maybe we should ask to see his license?' the blond cop went on. 'Shake them up a little bit.'

'Yeah,' the pimpled cop answered, 'maybe get a little you-know-what for ourselves. Little piece of coon-tang.'

Both cops laughed. Then the young cop caught a glimpse of Peewee, rising for breath from Wendell's embrace.

'Man!' he said. 'Would you look at that face! I've seen ugly women, but that one is *ugly*. Surprised she don't scare the livestock.'

'Yeah,' the blond cop agreed. 'I guess I'd just as soon go home to my wife.'

The disappointed cops drove off fast, spraying gravel, and as their taillights vanished, Wendell relaxed his grip on Peewee. The little man was sweating from a mixture of anxiety and indignation.

'Ooooh, man,' he said, 'Wendell, you got any idea what would have happened if they'd decided to check us out?'

Wendell reached under the dashboard and pulled out a pistol. 'I had me a pretty good idea,' he said, 'of what I'd have done if there was an emergency situation. And I also have a pretty good idea that you better find us another drop. We aren't going to be coming back here for some long time.'

'Scott, you never fail to surprise me,' said Peewee, offering a cigar.

And that makes it mutual, thought Wendell. He lighted the cigar and yawned. The long day had begun to catch up with him.

'Peewee,' he said, 'tell you what. You drive us home. And make sure that you go real slow.' He crawled over into the back seat. Long before they reached home, he had put out the cigar and gone to sleep.

VII

A few days later, Wendell drove his cab down to Albert Jackson's garage on the south side of Danville. He parked out back, wondering where the red-and-black Mercury was concealed.

He approached the front office on foot. 'Colored restroom's out back, boy,' said the attendant. 'Same way you come.'

Albert Jackson emerged from the garage. 'Hey, man,' he said, 'come on in.' He looked closely at Wendell. 'Never got a look at you in the daytime before,' he added. 'You Scott, right?'

They shook hands.

'Man,' Jackson went on, 'you're sure being talked about! Story about you and Peewee fooling the police is one of the funniest things I ever heard!' He smacked his thigh as he laughed. 'Still's still going, though, and so is my Merc. That what you come to have a look at?'

Wendell nodded. This little red-headed guy's a lot like Peewee, he thought with amazement. Maybe all bootleggers were some sort of kin.

The Merc was under a tarp in the darkest corner of the garage. Jackson uncovered it and explained the double transmission system in great detail. Wendell suggested a few improvements of his own devising, and Jackson nodded in agreement. 'Going to get yourself some more cars?' he asked. 'You better, 'cause the cops are going to know that Hudson right soon, if they don't know it now.'

'Got me a line on a couple of them already. Few more trips into the hills in the Hudson, and I'll be able to start me a fleet.' Wendell laughed. 'Always figured I'd be rich enough to own a fleet of cars some day, but I figured they'd be taxis!'

Jackson gave him some pointers. 'Thing to do,' he said, 'is keep your cars scattered all over the place. Reason I keep the Merc here, it's kind of like a pet, what with the two gearboxes and all. But I'm going to fix me up some others the same way. And get yourself some false plates. I got a friend in the state pen who makes them – I'll get you some. And out-of-state plates is always good, unless you're around one of those dinky little speed-trap towns. And any old plates that are the right color for this year. Wait a minute.'

Jackson unlocked a wall cupboard and showed Wendell a stack of license plates of all descriptions. The top ones said 'New Jersey'. Goddamn, thought Wendell, this man is an artist!

He felt inspired. 'Hey, man,' he said, 'you know what'd be funny? Let's look at the brake-light connections and see if we can figure out a switch so you could disconnect them from the dashboard. Think of it, dark country road at night, police right behind you, and you hit a fork in the road and just disappear. Leave them sitting in the dust and scratching their asses.'

Jackson guffawed and reached for his tool box. By the end of the afternoon, Wendell's invention was working fine, and both men were as happy as kids with a new toy train.

'Do you a turn someday, Scott,' said Jackson, as they got cleaned up.

'Hell, you already done me a turn with those two transmissions,' said Wendell. 'Going to use that little trick as soon as I can.'

He waved as he left the garage. Think I'll drive over by Leffert's and pick me out my next moonshine car, he thought. He remembered that he was also a taxi driver. Hell, he thought, too late to go by Leffert's today, anyhow. Might as well go back downtown and see if I can pick me up a fare.

Wendell had reached the bus depot when he saw her, standing in front of an office building on the opposite side of the street. It took him about one second to size this girl up as absolutely the best looking lady he had ever laid eyes on, in Danville or out of it. Her arms were full of packages, and she seemed to be looking for a taxi. And goddamn if there wasn't old Pops Foster in his wheezing old Buick, bearing down on her. Wendell pulled a bootleg turn that scared even him, and beat Pops to the girl by an inch.

'Taxi, miss?' he said, pulling up to the curb.

'Where did *you* come from?' asked the girl.

Pops Foster began to lean on the horn. 'That's my fare, Scott!' he shouted.

Wendell jumped out of the Lincoln, grabbed the girl's packages, and threw them in the front seat of his cab. Still ignoring Pops, he held the rear door open for the girl to enter, closed the door after her carefully, and resettled himself in the driver's seat. He made a quick check in the rear-view mirror. Whew! She was as gorgeous as he had thought. Wendell vowed right then that she was going to be his woman, if he had to make a million suicidal U-turns and antagonize every other taxi driver in Danville.

They were several blocks down Main Street before he remembered to inquire, 'Where to, miss?'

'I thought you'd never ask,' said the girl, who had quietly been enjoying the whole scene. 'I'd like to go out to Clearwater Road, please.'

'That's way out in the country,' Wendell said, not wanting the conversation to flag.

'I know it,' explained the girl patiently. 'I live there.'

'That's *way* out in the country,' Wendell said. I sound like a damn fool, he told himself. He tried another tack. 'You sure don't look like a country girl!' Oh God, that sounded fresh, and if there was one thing clear about this girl, it was that she was a lady. 'I'm actually a country boy myself,' he added. 'City's just a place to make some money and then get out.'

'You sure you a taxi driver?' asked the girl. 'You just went through a red light.'

By the time they reached Clearwater Road, Wendell had established that her name was Mary Jones and that she worked as a secretary for a young lawyer. The tone of her voice made him scent a rival there. Also, she usually took the bus, but had been doing some shopping that kept her in town. She was usually off at five.

The conversation with Mary Jones was not easy for Wendell. He seemed to fall all over his own tongue. Like a school kid, he thought. Like a damn mooncalf! But hell, Mary Jones was something else. She wasn't like those French girls, or like Sissy Carter, and she sure as hell wasn't like those ladies at Sweets'. *Whatever* it took, he was going to see more of her.

As he brooded about these matters, Mary Jones tapped him on the shoulder. 'That big white farmhouse on the left, please,' she said.

Wendell parked the cab in front of a freshly painted picket fence, opened the door for the girl, and scooped her parcels out of the front seat.

'Never you mind,' she said. 'My daddy'll help me with those. How much do I owe you?'

'Forget it,' said Wendell. 'Now, just you let me carry these bundles up to your doorstep.'

But she had her purse open, and she looked determined. Wendell was forced to name the fare and to balance the packages – damn, they were heavy! What was she buying, bricks? – on the hood of the taxi while he took her money and made change. When the front door of the house opened and Mary Jones's daddy came out, he surrendered the packages to him without a fight. Goddamn, he was a big man! Could probably carry the whole taxi into the house if he wanted to.

'Pleasure meeting you, miss,' he said to Mary Jones. 'Hope to run into you again.'

'Thank you,' said Mary Jones. That was all. Just 'Thank you.'

But Wendell knew, beyond the shadow of any doubt, that he would most certainly run into her again. He was going to make it his business. And for all her disinterest, she was standing at the picket fence and watching him as he drove away. He could see her in the rear-view mirror.

He sang to himself as he drove back toward the city, feeling good. He had things to do. Take most of the seats out of the Hudson, make another trip into the hills tonight, and forget about hanging around the depot, looking like a taxi driver. But in the days ahead, he was sure going to be cruising Main Street at five o'clock, looking for Mary Jones.

VIII

Wendell spent his mornings sleeping, his afternoons modifying a variety of old cars from Leffert's, and his nights coasting through the dark mountains. After his first adventurous evening, nothing much happened. No one chased him or shot at him, and Wendell, driving his heavily laden heaps through the dark country nights, sometimes found himself wishing for something to happen, just so he could get in a little road racing. Business was good. He was making money, doing well, and if Grandma Scott and Momma knew what he was up to, they weren't saying anything. But they weren't the kind of women who'd try to dictate to him anyhow. His grandma might reprimand him for taking the Lord's name in vain, but she knew that she couldn't slow him down. Once in a while she'd say something about his daddy, whom Wendell could not remember, but he seemed to have been a pretty fast-moving man, too.

Wendell managed to pick Mary up, 'by accident', a couple of times a week. As he regained some of his natural brashness, she seemed not to know quite what to make of him – clearly, she'd led a sheltered life. But then she began to relax and to give as good as she got. Soon they'd given up all pretense of 'accident', and she was simply waiting for him in front of her office building every evening. Wendell wondered what her smart-ass lawyer boss thought of *that*. And Wendell knew that he was going to marry her. No question about it.

There were still some formalities to be got through, however. One Friday, when he picked Mary up after work, she informed him that her parents wanted to meet him. That Sunday.

'My folks are getting suspicious,' Mary said. 'They

know I can't afford to take a taxi home every day. And I've been telling them all about you.'

Wendell's heart sank. The one look he had had at Mr Jones had been enough to scare him badly. He knew he had to meet Mary's family sooner or later, but Sunday was only two days away. This innocent-looking girl had ambushed him. He thought of all the excuses he could make that might put the dreaded day off for another week. Another date? No, either he'd have to explain in detail, or it would make Mary sore. Sick? Not the thing anyone would look for in a son-in-law, especially if he accidentally hit on something really bad. Poor eyesight? Deafness? Either could have kept him out of the army, but they weren't enough to keep him from meeting the Joneses. Maybe he could accidentally shoot himself in the foot. No, that'd take too much explaining.

He finally said the only thing that he could. 'What time on Sunday?'

'They're expecting you about one o'clock,' Mary said.

Expecting me, thought Wendell. Oh, shit!

Sunday was a long time in coming, and it dawned unexpectedly hot, more like August than late October. By the time Wendell pulled up in front of the big white house on Clearwater Road, his pants had lost their crease, his shirt had wilted, and his tie had almost dissolved.

Mary opened the door, looking fresh as a goddamn daisy. She always did, of course, but today there was absolutely no excuse for it. She led him into the steaming parlor, where her parents were waiting.

Mrs Jones smiled brightly as introductions were made, but Mr Jones was something else. Wendell knew why he had been reminded of the army – his first fleeting impression had been right on the nose. General Patton had nothing on the way this man could conduct a close-order inspection. And this man was one hell of a lot bigger than General Patton.

The hand-shaking over – Wendell had barely managed not to wince under Mr Jones's grasp – they all sat down and waited for someone to say something. The silence was occasionally broken by giggles as a small brother or sister, banned from this grown-up event, peeked around the door jamb. Mrs Jones shooed them out, but Wendell would have welcomed the diversion.

Mr Jones sat like a block of granite, and talked just about as much. Mrs Jones sat looking cool and refined. Nobody sweated except Wendell. Goddamn it, didn't these people have sweat glands?

He tried to talk about the weather. 'Hot, isn't it?' was about the best he could come up with, and Mr Jones's appearance, as he sat there all buttoned up in his heavy jacket, immediately gave it the lie. But goddamn it, it *was* hot. Were these people human? Wendell began to doubt even Mary.

Mary asked polite questions about his taxi business. He bluffed his way through, telling lies about how great it was. But that brought up something else that added to his discomfort – it wouldn't be too much longer before he'd have to tell Mary what he really did for money. And then, goddamn it, just as if sweating like a pig and having a bad conscience weren't enough, Wendell's stomach began to grumble loudly. Come to think of it, it *was* dinnertime. Didn't these people eat? Wasn't it enough that they didn't sweat? Wasn't he invited for dinner? Maybe he should have asked his mother to pack him sandwiches and coffee.

As if in answer to his prayers, Mrs Jones announced that she thought that dinner must be about ready. Wendell could have kissed her. She must have looked a whole lot like Mary when she was younger, he thought, as she disappeared into the dining room. Mary followed her.

Now Mr Jones and he were left to have a man-to-man talk. They stared at each other. Wendell tried to think of something to say about crops. After what seemed about two years, they were summoned to the dining room.

'Don't the menfolk look handsome,' Mary chirped as they entered. Wendell looked like hell, and he knew he looked like hell.

'Your daddy looks real distinguished,' he told Mary glumly.

He felt better when he saw the food on the table. There was a big Virginia ham, and mashed potatoes, and black-eyed peas, and greens, and a big platter of rolls. And an enormous, sweating pitcher of cold lemonade to go with it. Wendell put his napkin in his lap and reached for a roll.

Mrs Jones grabbed for his hand, and then Mary grabbed his other hand, the one with the roll in it. He dropped the roll, wondering what in hell was going on. A quick glance around the table showed him. They were now all holding hands, and every head except his was bowed. They were going to say grace! Wendell quickly bowed his head.

'Let us pray,' Mr Jones intoned. 'O Lord, we thank you for this bountiful table set before us, and for these, the foods of thy earth. For your blessing of our land and our home, we give thanks to you. Praise the Lord! Amen!'

With all that good food to eat, it wasn't necessary to try to talk. Wendell did most truly thank the Lord for that bountiful table. But dinner couldn't last forever.

The women cleared away, leaving the men to talk. Wendell felt less nervous. The food had lifted his spirits.

'What did you do in the war, Mr Scott?' Mr Jones asked.

Wendell gave a description of his army service that fell about halfway between what he told his mother and grandma and what he told his buddies. Mr Jones seemed a little less than satisfied, but he didn't actually disapprove. After all, Wendell *had* served his country, even if he'd only been a mechanic. What the hell did he expect? wondered Wendell. There sure weren't any black generals that he'd ever heard of.

'What you going to do besides this taxi service?' Mr Jones asked next. 'Can't be too good of a thing in a town like Danville.'

Goddamn it, thought Wendell, the man had seen right through the boastful lies about how great the taxi business was. What would happen, he wondered, if I told him I was the wildest-assed bootlegger in the whole county and was going to make myself one million dollars that way? Probably wouldn't believe that, either and certainly wouldn't approve.

'Might save my money and open a garage or service station,' he said.

'Too many of them already,' said Mr Jones.

Wendell wondered: what if I told him I'm going to

save my money and buy me a racing car and run every other damn thing right off the track? He'd already told Mary that part of his plan. She hadn't quite come out and said that she thought he was crazy, but her daddy probably would. Better not mention that, either.

Mary came back into the room. 'Wendell,' she said, 'we better get going if we going to get to that movie on time.'

He hadn't known that they were going to the movies, but the idea was fine with him. He said goodbye to Mary's parents and got her out of the house. When they reached the cab, he opened the front door for her. It was the first time she'd ever sat right up there beside him, and he was proud to be seen with her.

'My mother liked you,' said Mary.

'She's a nice lady,' said Wendell. Neither of them mentioned Mary's father.

Back in town, they passed the Danville Motor Speedway sign. Okay, thought Wendell, the movies are fine for tonight, but now that it looked like he and Mary were formally courting, he'd take her to the stock car races next week, and maybe she'd feel the excitement of what he had to do.

In the back of the balcony of Danville's only movie house, the part reserved for colored, Wendell slipped his arm around Mary's shoulders. It was the first time he had ever really touched her. The next day, for the life of him, he couldn't remember what picture they'd seen.

IX

Now Mary always sat in the front seat when Wendell drove her home in his taxi at night.

Once in a while she talked about Joe Robinson, the lawyer she worked for. Wendell's guess had been right – Robinson *was* sweet on her. Wendell also suspected that if Robinson made any formal move, Mr Jones would find nothing at all wrong with a lawyer, especially one who had been to school up north, as a prospective son-in-law. Still, it tickled him to think how pissed off Robinson must get, watching him drive off with Mary each evening. But Wendell knew he'd better get moving, all the same.

Every Sunday after the meeting with her family, he took Mary to the Speedway. The promoter had recently installed a small 'colored' section, and it wasn't a bad place to court, since they were nearly always almost alone. The white sections of the stands were packed with beer-drinking good old boys and their women, but it seemed that black people didn't care much for the auto races. Wendell thought all that would change once he got a chance to get on that track.

One Sunday, at the track, he decided it was time he and Mary had a serious talk about a lot of things.

'Mary,' he said, 'honey, you know I want to race. And we both know I can do it, soon as I get me a car. But Mary, honey, there is something else that maybe you don't know. I'm going to get me the money for that car, but my taxi business isn't going to be able to pay for it.' Wendell paused, wondering if she knew what he was trying to tell her. Well, one way or the other, there was just no help for it.

'Mary, honey,' he began again, 'you might as well know that . . . oh shit – excuse me! – you might as well know that I make most of my living running moonshine for Mr Henry Simms.' There, he'd said it. He didn't dare look at her.

She didn't laugh, and she didn't cry. When she finally spoke, all she said was, 'I know. I may just be a country girl, but I hear those souped-up cars going by in the night. And I always wonder if you're driving one of them. But Wendell, it's dangerous, and I worry. Reckon I always will worry. I'll worry when you're racing, too.'

Wendell couldn't believe his ears. She was not only accepting it, but she was talking like she'd already made up her mind that they'd always be together, so that she'd always have to worry about him.

'You wouldn't mind being the wife of a bootlegger?' he asked.

He'd hardly gotten the words out of his mouth before she threw her arms around him and gave him a big kiss.

'You wouldn't mind being the wife of a *race driver?*' Wendell sounded jubilant.

'Oh, Wendell,' Mary said, 'I'd be proud to be the wife of a race driver. So proud.' She began to cry.

Wendell wanted to go right down onto that track, stop the race, and tell everyone that Mary Jones was going to marry *him*. He grabbed her, and they kissed again, at length. It was some time before they looked around to find themselves the center of attention and comment, some of it pretty raw. Mary blushed to the tips of her ears.

'Let's get out of here,' Wendell said. 'You got to meet my mother and Grandma. I been telling them a lot about you.'

The three women liked each other on sight, and Mary began stopping by at the Scott house whenever she had the chance. Grandma Scott was especially taken with Wendell's choice. Wendell was tickled. Ever comes to a fair fight, he speculated, my grandma can probably lick her daddy.

They hadn't told Mr Jones yet, and they couldn't think of any way to break it to him gently. Wendell had been hanging around the Jones house as much as he could stand to, and he knew Mrs Jones was fond of him, and hell, the little kids were easy to buy off with candy. But Mary's father remained something else again.

Wendell suggested they just go off to a justice of the peace and get married and tell Mr Jones later. But Mary wanted to do it right, a church wedding with a white dress, and she wasn't going to let Wendell's fear of her father cheat her out of it.

Wendell finally agreed to just come straight out and ask Mr Jones's permission to marry Mary. So the next Sunday, dressed in his best clothes, he set out in his cab for the Joneses' house. His face was covered with tiny nicks from his razor, and he had to admit that he was nervous. It was one hell of a lot easier outracing the Danville police with a carload of illegal hooch than it was to face this God-fearing *big* man.

He parked the Lincoln by the picket fence, and the minute he got out he felt like a thousand eyes were on him. A small child – Wendell couldn't make out which one – had been posted on guard and withdrew from the window as he approached the porch. Goddamn, he thought, everybody but Mr Jones must know what today's all about, right down to the littlest of them. He had just raised his hand to knock at the door when it flew open as if my magic. Malicious giggles rose from behind it as Mary arrived to shoo Benjamin, Isaac, Betty Lou, and May – all previously, if ineffectively, bribed – out of the way.

Mary led Wendell to the front parlor. They sat on the sofa, a decorous distance apart. The kids popped their heads into the room, laughed like maniacs, and disappeared again.

'Sure is nice being here alone with you,' Wendell observed.

'Now you just be still and don't fret. We got the whole day ahead of us. The folks is out back – they'll be with us in a while. You just sit there. You look real nice today, Mr Scott.'

He had hoped for a five-minute conversation with Mr Jones, after which he could grab Mary's hand and head for the races at the Speedway. Clearly, it wasn't going to be that easy.

And Mary, Wendell thought, looked about as pretty today as he could have imagined. But he couldn't get within three feet of her. Every time he began to move across the sofa toward her, there was another damn giggling kid. Once Betty Lou just opened one door, skipped right across the room, and out another door. Wendell normally liked the kids, got along with them fine, but today he was about ready to start wringing necks.

'Honey,' he said to Mary. 'I know this real nice justice of peace, man name of Nate Rackley. Does a little bootlegging on the side.'

Mary laughed, 'I'm sure Daddy's really going to approve if you and I go off and get married by some bootlegger.' She turned solemn again. 'Moonshine is something we never mention in this house, Wendell. We don't make it, drink it, or think it. So you know just what to tell Daddy about your taxi business.'

She must have put in a good word for me, Wendell thought. Just wonder how much good it'll do compared with Mr Robinson's fancy law degree.

When Mr Jones came into the parlor, Wendell shot up off the sofa like a rocket, his hand extended stiffly, and tried to produce a casual, friendly smile. He felt his face freeze into a dumb-ass grin, and wondered if he had remembered to shine his shoes. It was too late to look now, though.

'Good afternoon, sir.' Wendell felt his palms beginning to sweat. 'Sure is nice weather we're having.'

'Go on and sit back down,' said Mr Jones.

'Excuse me,' said Mary, 'I think I hear Momma calling me.' She left the room.

The two men looked at each other for what seemed like a year to Wendell. Might as well get right down to it, he thought. Mr Jones was clearly in no hurry to speak – probably never had been in his whole life.

Wendell cleared his throat. 'Well, now, sir,' he began. 'Uh, I want to – that is, I'm asking your permission – uh, I want to marry your daughter. I mean, both of us, Mary and me, want to get married. To each other, you understand. I've known your daughter for some time now, and I most surely do respect her. Fact of the matter is, I love your daughter, and she's the only woman in the whole world for me. I could provide for her. I work hard. I never spent time in jail. I'll be a good husband. I own my own cab' – it was getting all mixed up, Wendell thought –

'and someday I'm going to own a whole lot of them and' – he ended somewhat lamely – 'well, me and Mary want to get married. With your permission, sir, of course.'

He'd said it. He hadn't said it very well, but he'd said it. Looking down at the parlor rug, Wendell noticed for the first time that it had a real pretty floral pattern. He lifted his head at a strange sound.

Mr Jones was laughing.

Wendell hadn't supposed the man capable of it, and he sat transfixed, just staring, as Mary's father swayed back and forth, his huge frame shaking.

'Hold it, son, hold it right there,' Mr Jones gasped.

That does it, thought Wendell. He thinks this is so comical, it looks like I'll just have to kidnap Mary.

'My wife and I,' said Mr Jones, recovering a bit of his usual ponderous style, 'would be right proud to have you for a son-in-law.'

Wendell was dumbfounded. Had he heard right? Then it began to dawn on him – that 'my wife and I' stuff. There must have been a lot of conversation going on that Wendell didn't know about, and Mary must have done her part in it real well.

'You would?' said Wendell. 'Well I'll be damned! Excuse me, sir.'

Mary's father walked to the parlor door and opened it. There were Mary, her mother, and all the little kids. They all threw their arms around Wendell at once.

X

Ever since he heard that Wendell and Mary were going to get married, Peewee had been planning the bachelor party to end all bachelor parties. His main man wasn't going to go off into domestic bliss without one hell of a send-off. The event was scheduled for two days before the wedding, since Peewee was going to be Wendell's best man as well. He was taking his responsibilities seriously and had vowed not to touch one single drink for at least twenty-four hours before the ceremony.

The party was, of course, to be held at Sweets'.

Grandma Scott watched Wendell as he tied his tie before the bathroom mirror, wearing his Sunday best. 'Just don't you be carrying on,' she warned him. 'No messing around. I know what these bachelor parties are like, and I told Mary I'd caution you. Told her that you'd better listen to me. And you'd better!'

'Hey, Grandma,' said Wendell, 'how do you know what a bachelor party is like? You been to one? You been one of those naked ladies that jumps out of the cake?'

The old lady could still move pretty fast. She took a series of whacks at him with a towel, connecting about three times out of four, as Wendell fled through the living room and out the front door. 'Hush your mouth,' she shouted. 'I know a lot more than you think. I know about the carrying-on and the boozing and the women!'

'Sounds good, Grandma,' Wendell shouted back, grinning, as he started the Hudson and shot out of the driveway.

Sweets' was already jumping when he got there. Funny, he thought, it wasn't all that long ago that I came here to meet Simms, didn't know a soul, and now just about every face is familiar. And I'm here for fun tonight, not to transact business, but I sure do know a lot more about what kind of business is getting carried on. He waved a hand around the room. A couple of the men with the big pinky rings – colleagues now, if not friends – and almost every lady in the place smiled or winked or waved back at him.

At the edge of the dance floor, six tables had been pushed together. They were covered with white cloths, an elegance almost unheard-of for Sweets'. Peewee and Simms were seated at the center of a noisy group that included Leroy Wiggins and other friends from around town. A sign on the wall behind the tables announced 'The Wendell Scott Buy Your Booze at the Bar Bachelor Party'. It looked to Wendell like a whole lot of booze had already been consumed – everyone at the tables appeared to have a pretty big head start on him. He remembered his homecoming party, with its table full of food. Not even a spare rib here tonight, he thought, but bottles from here to the moon.

Wendell walked over to the party and sat down quietly before anyone noticed him. Then Peewee saw him and stood up and started to applaud, and then everyone else was standing and shouting and applauding and whistling. One or two of the other customers glared as the jukebox was droned out.

'We're taking over this club, and we ain't leaving,' Peewee shouted defiantly. It would have been more impressive if he'd been standing on a chair, but the idea had come to him too late, and he wasn't steady enough to manage it.

It took Wendell a couple of hours to catch up to his friends, but he was feeling mellow as could be by the time things started up between Simms and Peewee. At first he didn't quite catch on to what was happening.

Peewee was just rising to propose the thirtieth toast. The last several had been mostly addressed to himself – 'To the best-looking man in Danville, Virginia,' and stuff like that – and everybody was getting a little tired of it but no one had complained. 'I propose a toast!' said Peewee, slurring his words slightly.

Simms just looked down into his glass and said, 'Oh man, you just shut up with your toasts.'

'Look, man,' said Peewee, 'I'm the host of this affair, ain't I? Well then, it's up to me to see that the toasts keep flowing freely.'

'Your mouth's what's flowing freely,' said Simms. His tone was ugly, and even Peewee, who didn't take lip from anybody, was forced to consider.

'Don't you be talking to me like that, Simms,' he said seriously. 'My man Scott's getting married Sunday, and if I want to propose a toast to the bride and groom, ain't nobody, especially you, going to stop me.'

'Okay, okay,' said Simms. 'But stand up when you propose a toast.'

'I am standing up, wise-ass,' said Peewee. 'I got a good mind to take you outside.'

Only Wendell was sober enough to realize what a rash statement this was. 'Okay, man, stay cool,' he advised Peewee. 'Let's stick to the business at hand, like toasting *me*.'

'All right, Wendell,' Peewee said, 'I just want you to know that all of us, even this mean dude Simms – '

Simms interrupted. 'What do you mean "even"? I got a good mind to cut you, boy.'

Peewee ignored this and started all over again. 'I want to propose a toast,' he said, 'to Wendell Scott and his lovely bride.' As his audience burst into applause, he raised his glass, sipped, and immediately began to choke helplessly. 'Man, this stuff is piss!' he said. 'What'd they put in this drink?'

Leroy Wiggins sniffed the offending glass. 'That's ice water, you dumb ass,' he said. 'You just drank straight chaser.'

Even Simms joined in the general laughter.

'Now,' said Leroy to Peewee, 'why don't you give Wendell his going-away present?'

'What are you talking about?' asked Wendell. 'I'm not going anywhere. I'm just going to stay right here in Sweets' until they come and carry me away.'

'Listen, man,' said Peewee. 'You're getting married. You're going up to that preacher, and you're saying "I do," and you're leaving your life as a wild-assed cat behind you. You're going away all right. But some of us boys got together to get you a little wedding present, a little something for you to remember us by.'

Leroy, impatient, stood up, turned to the bar, and yelled, 'Hey, Alma! Luanne! Get yourselves over here.'

The two girls had been sitting at the bar, smoking cigarettes and drinking glasses of sweet red wine. They had been ignoring the bachelor party – and, for a change, the rest of the customers. Now, like a well-rehearsed sister act, they swung their stools around, descended, and began to walk across the room nice and slow, wiggling their tails. They were big girls, both of them, known and admired even beyond Sweets'.

Wendell realized that they were for him. Some present! After tonight, he thought, I'll be the most faithful man in the world – but tonight, Lord forgive me! My God, just look at them! Three hundred pounds between them, easy, and all of it in the right places. He wondered how he would have managed if his friends had been able to afford three such girls.

When the girls came up, Wendell rose and put an arm around each one. 'Gentlemen,' he announced, 'I want to take this occasion to thank you one and all. You surely have touched my heart.'

'Man, we touched *something*,' Peewee observed as the girls snuggled up. The other guests laughed.

'And now,' said Wendell, 'if you gentlemen will excuse me, I got some pressing business to attend to outside. And thanks again. You-all sure know how to make a man happy. This is just about the best present I ever got. Maybe I should get married more often.'

To a chorus of cheers and applause, he led Alma and Luanne across the dance floor. He had the feeling that the two girls could easily carry him on their shoulders if they wanted to. Maybe he should ask them. Bowing them out the door into the fresh night air, he led them on to the Hudson. They were startled to find it partially loaded up with moonshine.

'You planning to work tonight?' asked Luanne. 'We thought this was your bachelor party, your night to have a little fun.'

'Got one drop to make,' said Wendell, 'then we'll have ourselves all the fun there is.'

The girls seemed resigned. They crawled into the loaded car and stretched themselves out on the cases of moonshine. Luanne opened a case, then a bottle, and took a sizeable swig. Alma tickled Wendell's ear. He started the engine, and the Hudson, with its load of booze and fast women, pulled out of Sweets' parking lot. Grandma should see me now, Wendell thought.

XI

It didn't take Wendell long to discover that the girls were easily bored. Just drinking and looking at the scenery wasn't enough for them. 'Come on, lover boy,' Alma pouted, 'you don't figure on driving all night long?' It was only two minutes since they had left Sweets'.

Alma pressed herself against Wendell's arm. When she reached for his thigh, she found that Luanne's hand was already there. Damn, thought Wendell, it's a good thing that there's *not* three of them. He couldn't tell who it was that was beginning to unbutton his shirt. He had to push someone out of the way to change gears.

It must have been Alma that he'd pushed. 'What's the matter, honey, ain't I pleasing you?' she said.

'I thought we were going to have us some excitement,' complained Luanne. Alma had, in turn, pushed her toward the door of the car. Jars of moonshine rattled beneath the shift in weight.

'We going to have some excitement as soon as I make this drop,' said Wendell. Acting the host, he asked, 'You ladies want to see my gearshift?'

Alma giggled and reached for his crotch. She was surprised when Wendell switched on the dome light and removed her grasping hand. By God, he was really going to show them some damn piece of machinery, she thought. Oh, well, Peewee'd given them a whole lot of money, and if this was this cat's idea of fun, okay.

Alma feigned interest as Wendell pointed out the two transmissions. 'What's they for, honey?' she asked. 'I ain't never seen anything like them.'

'Got one for running forward, one for running backward,' Wendell explained.

'Backwards?' she repeated, with a flicker of genuine curiosity.

'Show you ladies later,' Wendell said, turning off the interior light.

'Ummm.' Luanne took another hit off the bottle. 'I can hardly wait.' She was getting depressed.

Wendell was now driving through the quiet residential neighborhoods of the black section of Danville. Nearly there, he thought, as he approached his customer's house. He was cruising along quiet and easy when a patrol car that had been parked on a side road switched on its lights and drew into the street in front of him.

Wendell threw the car into reverse. It jumped like a jackrabbit, throwing Alma and Luanne into a tangled heap as Wendell ran through the gears, picking up speed. He negotiated a corner, still going backwards and faster than hell. Two more cop cars lighted up behind him – it seemed like they'd got the whole countryside staked out. As he rammed the Hudson into forward gear, the first patrol car, in hot pursuit, turned the corner. Wendell, picking up speed, barely missed it. The patrol car, swerving to avoid a head-on crash, ended up in someone's front yard.

Wendell was now cold sober. He knew exactly what he was going to do. He even had time for courtesy. 'Everything all right, ladies?' he asked Alma and Luanne.

They were clinging to each other for dear life. This crazy-assed dude was fixing to get them all killed! They sure as hell hadn't bargained with old Peewee for anything like this!

'Hang on, ladies,' said Wendell. 'We're going to have us a little action just as soon as we lose us a couple of patrol cars.' He made a gut-tearing turn, heading for the new white suburbs, where the new houses were just going up on wide streets. He braked slightly on a sharp turn, and the police behind him, seeing his lights, braked, too.

Wendell was now running through the new public park. The road had just been bulldozed, was not even paved yet. There were still thick woods on either side. It looked like a straight downhill run from here, but Wendell knew that it wasn't. He reached out to the dashboard and flicked the switch that disconnected his brake lights, the switch that Albert Jackson and he had worked out. Gauging his speed and distance carefully, he braked hard, then took a sharp left where the road swung around to circle the park. He slowed down to listen for the crash.

The two police cars, chasing the suddenly invisible Hudson, missed the turn and went straight off into the woods. Wendell heard the screech of brakes, then the crunch of metal on metal. He made a tight U-turn, and drove back up the hill. Alma and Luanne seemed about to revive, and he just wasn't able to resist carrying on a little. As he drove past the wrecked police cars, now surrounded by dazed but intact officers surveying the damage, he honked his horn three times.

'Open fire!' Wendell heard somebody yell. Man, he thought, I knew they'd be pissed off, but not *that* pissed off. 'Get your heads down, girls,' he cautioned Alma and Luanne. Then bullets started flying, and he stepped on the gas.

Five minutes later he was on the highway out of Danville, and across the county line. By the time he pulled off the road and into some bushes, Alma and Luanne didn't have any notion of where they were, and they didn't particularly care. They were still excited, though. This had been the joyride to end all joyrides, and while they thought that Wendell was most likely crazy, it was a craziness they could admire.

Wendell got out and looked at the car. Nothing seemed to be leaking, and there were no dents. Goddamn cops couldn't shoot any better than they could drive. He got back into the car, where Luanne was inspecting her face in a compact by the dome light, trying to look as if she did this sort of thing every night.

'Sure could use a drink,' Wendell said, and Alma handed him the open bottle. Despite all the speeding, not much of it had been spilled.

Wendell took a long swallow, and then the girls moved in on him, massaging his back and arms, removing his shirt. Big girls like that, it was a little bit like getting caught in a mangle, but he liked it just fine. Luanne had kicked off her high heels, and now Alma was shaking off her earrings. The cases of moonshine groaned beneath them as they rolled around. Somehow, in that cramped and loaded car, they were managing to get undressed. Alma chewed on Wendell's ear and whispered, 'Oooh, honey, you're my man.'

'Just wait till everybody hears about *this*,' said Luanne.

Wendell sat up like a jack-in-the-box. 'Hears about *what*?'

'Just never you mind, honey,' Luanne said, punching him back down. 'Nobody's going to hear anything.' She was unhooking her bra with one hand.

Wendell settled back to enjoy the rest of his party.

It was nearly daylight when they finally got themselves sorted out. Wendell drove back to Danville flat-out, tearing through the quiet dawn. The girls were still cooing like doves, but when he let them off, he knew he wouldn't see them again. He was going to be a married man in no time at all.

His customer was annoyed to be awakened so early – after all, he'd been up half the night waiting for the stuff to arrive – but Wendell didn't even think of apologizing. He went home and slept right through until Sunday morning, his wedding day.

BOOK II

I

They lived with Wendell's mother and grandma the first few months they were married, while they were building a house of their own. There was more room out at the Jones farm, of course, but it would have been impossible to hide Wendell's trips into the hills from Mr Jones if they'd all been living under the same roof.

Wendell had picked up a nice piece of land, a fairly good-sized lot near his grandma's house, and it was not entirely coincidental that a good-sized garage already stood on the property. As the house went up, the garage and the backyard began to fill with Wendell's cars, or parts of them. The Lincoln with 'Scott's Taxi Service' painted on the door was always right out front. Although the money Wendell made from hauling liquor was much greater than what he could make from the cab, the taxi provided a good front, and Wendell needed one. The cops were getting a whole lot better at catching moonshiners, and although they hadn't got Wendell, a lot of his colleagues had gone off to jail. He'd had to get rid of the Hudson, which seemed a shame – there had been some good times in that car.

He was out tinkering under a Ford one morning, shortly after they'd moved into the newly finished house, when Mary brought him some coffee. Wendell heard her approaching footsteps. 'Hey, hand me that wrench, will you?' he said.

'Hay is for horses,' Mary replied.

'I'm sorry, honey,' he said, crawling out from under the car. 'I thought you were Peewee.'

'Here's your coffee,' Mary said, handing it to him.

'Isn't it about dinnertime?' Wendell asked.

'Not for a while yet,' Mary said. Then she burst out,

half teasing, half really mad. 'Wendell, you don't even know where the time goes when you're fooling around with these things. I swear, once you crawl under one of these damn cars, you could be gone for days before you'd notice it. We been married for four months now, and some days about all I get to see of you is the soles of your feet!'

'Aw, come on, honey, I just – ' He broke off, noticing the look on her face. 'What are you smiling about, woman?'

'I went to see Dr Thompson this morning.'

'What for? What's wrong?' Wendell was concerned, but Mary was still smiling.

'Nothing's wrong. Nothing at all! Oh, Wendell, can't you guess?'

He looked at her. Her eyes were sparkling, and it seemed, now he thought of it, like she was a little plumper, her waist a little more rounded. 'You went to Doc Thompson and nothing was wrong,' he repeated, trying for time to take it all in.

'Yes, Wendell, that's right,' Mary said with mock solemnity. Sometimes she sounded like her Daddy, he thought. The two ideas came together in his mind.

'You're going to have a baby,' he said. 'I'm going to be a daddy!'

He didn't drop the coffee – it fell right out his hand. He grabbed Mary and kissed her and whirled her around, laughing. 'Well,' he said, 'at least that proves you've been seeing something of me besides my feet!'

Mary gave him a good hard punch on the arm, and they kissed again.

'So I'm going to be a daddy,' Wendell repeated.

'That's right,' Mary said again. 'So I think that it's time you started thinking about settling down a little bit more. Maybe putting a little more thought into running that garage business and a little less thought into running liquor.'

'We'll see,' said Wendell, almost absent-mindedly. He was thinking of how delighted his mother and grandma were going to be when they heard. Hell, his grandma was going to be a *great*-grandma.

'It's going to be a boy,' he said.

'Of course it is,' said Mary. 'And he'll probably be able to drive before he can walk. But not moonshine cars.'

'He'll be a race driver,' Wendell laughed. Like his old man, he thought, if his old man ever gets to be one. With a baby coming, the dream might have to be postponed a little while longer, but he still knew what he was going to do.

He put his arm around Mary and began walking her toward the house. 'Now you tell me everything Doc Thompson said. We're going to have to start taking extra good care of you.'

'Just get me to the hospital in time,' said Mary. 'That'll be one time when you can probably go as fast as you want, and no policeman will try to stop you. And I'd like to go in the taxi, please.'

They were holding each other and laughing when Peewee came around the corner. When they told him the news he immediately suggested that they name the baby for him. After all, he'd been best man at their wedding, hadn't he?

II

It was no accident that Wendell's colleagues were going to jail. All over the South, local police were coming under increased pressure from state and Federal authorities to crack down on the illegal liquor trade. In Danville, Sheriff Cotten was being leaned on by Captain McNeill of the state police. It was Cotten who had given the order to shoot on the night of Wendell's bachelor party. He had been infuriated then, and he still got damn mad every time he thought about it. And McNeill drove him crazy. McNeill thought he was such hot shit in his goddamn military-style uniform. McNeill and his goddamn meetings. Strutting around and giving orders, as if that were all that needed to be done. A few more men and a lot more money from the state would be a whole lot better than more goddamn lip from McNeill, Cotten thought.

McNeill stood late one evening in Cotten's office at the Danville police headquarters, sticking little colored pins into a map of Danville. Cotten looked out of the window, wondering how long it would go on this time. He'd heard it all before, God knows.

'Damn it, I want action,' McNeill said. 'Them runners is making you-all look silly, and that makes *me* look bad. I want results, and I want them *now*!' He was becoming red in the face.

'Captain, my men do have other duties – ' Cotten began.

'And I don't want no excuses!' McNeill shouted. Obnoxious as only a little man can be, thought Cotten. He wondered vaguely if maybe McNeill had bribed someone to make the minimum height requirement. Maybe I could turn him in for that and get him off my neck, he thought. Or maybe I could just sort of be cleaning my gun and have it go off just by accident, shoot him right up the ass. He briefly pondered the penalty for involuntary manslaughter.

'I don't want any crybaby stories about not enough men and not enough money,' McNeill went on. 'One good cop could get the job done. And I do most particularly want to see the ass of that nigger runner – what's his name, Scott? – yes, I do *most* particularly want to see that black ass nailed to the barn door.'

Cotten winced. Scott was a thorn in his side, but he didn't bear him any personal grudge. No more than any other bootlegger who kept making him and his men look like monkeys.

'Captain McNeill,' he began patiently, keeping his voice level. 'I've got snitches, but I'm getting lousy information. And I've got the fastest cars in the state, but they aren't fast enough. Those runners must be using airplane engines. And as for Scott, I've got at least one man watching his place almost all the time. I've even had men up trees, watching the house with binoculars. But damn if that boy doesn't have cars stashed all over town. Don't know where he gets them. Hell, people must be *giving* them to him. He's already got a backyard full, looks like an automobile graveyard.'

McNeill was on his way out the door, and Cotten got there just in time to slam it behind him. Then he sat down at his desk and put his head in his hands. He was going to be breaking in a couple of rookies tonight; maybe he'd take them out after Scott. Damn it, if informers and surveillance and strategy couldn't catch the bastard, maybe beginners' luck could.

Cotten sent out for sandwiches and settled down at his desk with a book of crossword puzzles. He wasn't even going to think about Scott until the rookies reported in at ten p.m. When the two new men, Langer and Castle, arrived, he briefed them for a couple of minutes, then set out with them in a patrol car to cruise the black part of Danville. About as much chance of finding a bootlegger here as finding a needle in a haystack, Cotten thought. Still, it didn't hurt to try, and he might as well break Langer and Castle in nice and easy.

And then, Scott tooled by in an old Mercury. 'By God,

that's *him!*' Cotten shouted to the driver, Castle, who immediately jammed the accelerator pedal to the floor and hit the siren.

People ran out of their houses to see what the action was. Castle stayed close on the Mercury's tail, heading for the outskirts of town. 'Just stay cool,' Cotten instructed him. 'Just stay right with him until you can cut him off.'

Funny thing was, Scott wasn't driving very fast. Must be that he hasn't had time to soup up the Merc, Cotten thought, recollecting that he hadn't seen that car before. Tonight just might be the night. Langer drew his service revolver and looked inquiringly at Cotten, who nodded. Langer took aim and shot out both the Merc's rear tires.

Scott slowed, running on the rims, but keeping the car under control, then stopped, got out fast, and began to run. The patrolmen did not even have time to shout a warning. The crazy son of a bitch was running right at them! Scott charged the police car, ran right up over the hood, and disappeared into the bushes at the side of the road.

'Go get him, you stupid bastards,' Cotten shouted at the rookies. Castle and Langer almost fell out of the car and took up the chase. Cotten got out more slowly, wishing he were a younger man. He watched the two young cops lunge into the bushes, then heard cursing and cries of pain as they ran hard into a barbed-wire fence. Scott strolled out of the bushes, unmarked. 'Good evening, Sheriff,' he said.

Cotten didn't say anything. He walked over to Scott's Merc and looked inside. He looked in the trunk, for which Scott politely proffered the key. He even looked in the glove compartment. It was clean as a whistle. *There wasn't any goddamn moonshine in the whole goddamn car!*

'You'd better just go on, Scott,' Cotten said evenly. He moved back to the patrol car to join Castle and Langer, who had emerged from the underbrush looking as if they'd been locked up in a cage full of bobcats. 'We'll just talk about this later.'

Wendell drove off slowly toward the Jones farm, where Mary was visiting with her parents. He chuckled at the story he'd tell her on the way home. He was still riding his rear rims and he wondered if her daddy had any spare tires.

When the officer came to arrest Wendell the next day, the warrant specified 'suspicion of transporting illegal whiskey and assaulting a police officer'. Sheriff Cotten knew that getting it to stick was going to be a bitch, since no whiskey had been found. And, banged up and bandaged though they were, it was going to be damned hard to prove that Castle and Langer had been assaulted by anybody, except maybe each other. But a little harassment might not be a bad idea. A little revenge might be an even better one.

Wendell arrived at the station house at nine o'clock. Joe Robinson, Mary's lawyer friend, got there five minutes later. Cotten and Robinson conferred briefly in the sheriff's office, and then Robinson came out. 'Okay, Wendell,' he said, 'you can go right on home.'

He was cut short by Cotten. 'Look, Scott, we can't keep you this time. But you better watch it, 'cause, by God, I'm going to put your ass in a sling!'

'Yes, boss,' said Wendell.

'Don't give me that "yes, boss" crap,' Cotten shouted. '*Get out of my sight!*'

Langer and Castle had another brush with Wendell a couple of months later. This time he was driving Mary to the hospital, and the least they could do was give him a police escort. The next day he stopped by the station house to leave them a couple of cigars to celebrate the birth of Wendell, Jr.

III

McNeill never found out about the night Castle and Langer got caught in the barbed wire. That's all I'd need, thought Cotten. But the dumb bastard was on his way over to Danville for another of his insufferable briefings, and Cotten already knew every damn thing he was going to say. He was holding his head in his hands when McNeill marched in, without knocking.

'I want all your men in here, right now,' said McNeill.

'Right away, sir.' Cotten got up from his desk as slowly as he could, sauntered to the door, and stuck his head out. 'Hey, you guys, come on in here if you've got a minute,' he drawled.

McNeill didn't say anything; he just waited for the few patrolmen on duty in the station house to drift in and seat themselves on and around Cotten's desk. 'I've never seen a sorrier-looking lot of policemen,' he told Cotten. Good thing Langer and Castle aren't here, the sheriff thought. They were both still so covered with Band-Aids that it was hard to tell them apart.

McNeill walked over to the map of the city and began his briefing, sticking in his little colored pins. He must manufacture them, Cotten thought. The sheriff was always careful to pull out all the pins and put them in the ashcan the minute McNeill was off the premises, but McNeill always had a fresh supply.

McNeill stuck a red pin in the map, and Cotten stifled a yawn. 'Here,' McNeill began, 'is the home of the famous *Ne*-gro bootlegger, Mr Wendell Scott. As you must all be aware, gentlemen, on one occasion or the other Mr Scott has made goddamn jackasses of us all. Now, first of all, I think we should keep this house' – he pointed to the red pin – 'under constant surveillance.'

Cotten raised his hand.

'Do you wish to make a comment, Sheriff Cotten?' McNeill asked.

'Sir, we've had that house under twenty-four-hour-a-day, seven-day-a-week surveillance,' Cotten said. And how many times do I have to tell you that, you dumb-ass little shit, he added mentally. 'Moreover, sir,' he continued aloud, 'we have searched the house on several occasions, as well as the garage and every one of the cars both in the garage and in the backyard, and we have not found one drop of hootch. We just don't know where he puts the stuff.'

'What about the cars he's hauling with?' McNeill demanded. 'Can't your men even knock off some of those?'

'Sir,' volunteered a young cop with acne marks, 'we did get a couple of them a while ago. Blasted out the radiators with a twelve-gauge.' He turned to a young blond cop, his partner, and snickered.

'Yeah,' the blond cop added, 'but then the bastard went and started putting the engines in the *back* of the damn cars. What are you going to do with a smart-ass nigger like that?'

'We haven't tried land mines yet,' said Cotten.

McNeill looked for just a second as if he thought this might be a good idea, then said sternly, 'We can't do that. We might hurt some innocent women and children.'

McNeill brooded for a moment before he spoke again. 'Gentlemen,' he said, 'I think you should kill the bastard.'

There are days when I just might agree, thought Cotten, but first you've got to tell me how.

'Gentlemen,' said McNeill, 'I have a plan.'

Cotten could hardly wait to hear it. But McNeill did have a plan, and later that night Cotten found himself riding right along with him in the same patrol car, one of six that McNeill had commandeered for his purpose. Each car contained four armed men. As the convoy with McNeill in the lead left Danville and headed for the countryside, Cotten began wondering if McNeill was a maniac. Maybe he really did think he was General Eisenhower.

Beyond the city limits, McNeill ordered all headlights doused. The moon was bright enough to see by, and there wasn't much traffic in the country at this time of night.

'Now you just watch,' McNeill told Cotten. 'I know every liquor drop for miles around here, and tonight we're going to get us a bootlegger or two. Maybe even Mr Wendell Scott.' Cotten wondered why he was whispering. 'We're almost there,' McNeill went on. 'Get ready.' What does he expect me to do? Cotten thought.

McNeill was on the radio now, still whispering as he cautioned the men not to break formation and to move quietly. They drove past a big farmhouse, and a minute or two later, they spotted the parked car, standing all by its lonesome, about twenty feet away from a big haystack. McNeill got back on the radio and ordered the convoy to a halt. 'We're getting out,' he whispered. 'We're going to implement Plan A.'

What in hell is Plan A? Cotten thought, getting out with the three other men. He saw the glint of the revolver in McNeill's hand. Crazy bastard might kill somebody!

McNeill flattened himself in the dirt and began to crawl toward the parked car. Twenty-three men followed him. Cotten didn't crawl; he just stooped over a little bit. He was getting too old for this kind of thing.

At the rear of the procession, the cop with the acne nudged his blond partner. 'Hey,' he whispered, 'isn't this about where you and me caught those two niggers necking that night? That terrible ugly woman?'

'Sure is,' said the blond cop, tickled by the recollection.

McNeill suddenly stood up and blew his whistle, and all the men rushed forward. Cotten was near the front of the line, not because he was particularly enthusiastic about Plan A, but because he'd been in the first car. The men had the haystack and the car surrounded within seconds. Gun drawn, McNeill jerked open the door next to the driver's seat. The dome light went on just as he switched on his flashlight, so there was plenty of light for everyone to see.

What they saw was Danville's Mayor DuPree. 'Oh, my God!' said McNeill, still pointing his revolver at the mayor.

DuPree was cowering in the back seat of the car, naked as a jaybird. He wasn't alone, either. Cotten got a look at the young lady who was trying to conceal herself behind the mayor. He didn't recognize her, at least not the part of her that he could see, which was mostly rump. But even if she was one of the mayor's constituents, the sheriff was pretty sure she wasn't anything like old enough to vote. Son of a bitch! he thought.

The mayor was sitting up now, covering his crotch with his hands. There were still only bits and pieces to be seen of the girl. His Honor must be sitting on her, Cotten decided.

'It's Mayor DuPree!' the stunned McNeill announced to the assembled troops.

'Who the hell did you think it was, Harry S. Truman?' snarled the mayor. 'What in all hell is the meaning of this? Put out those damn lights!' The last was addressed to the two young cops, who had advanced with their flashlights to see what was happening. The lights were put out.

'Who's in charge here?' demanded the mayor, and McNeill meekly raised his hand.

DuPree peered at him. 'You're McNeill from the state police, aren't you, boy?' he said menacingly. 'What in hell are you doing out here, and with all my cops to boot?'

'Your Honor,' McNeill began humbly, 'one of my best informers told me that there was going to be a big liquor drop here tonight – '

The mayor cut him off. 'You goddamn well better fire that informer,' he said. 'And you goddamn well better be in my office first thing tomorrow morning.'

McNeill gave the naked mayor a sloppy salute, then did an about-face and ordered the men back to their cars. Moving slowly after him, Cotten thought that if all this was somebody's idea of a joke, it was by God a pretty good one!

IV

The same night the cops caught Mayor DuPree, Wendell went to the movies. Mary wanted to come along.

'Oh, no, honey,' he tried to dissuade her. 'One baby to take care of all day and another on the way, you're going to be too tired.'

'Am not,' Mary said. 'Look, I can get the supper dishes done in two minutes. We can just load up the baby and take him right along with us.'

Wendell explained that she couldn't go because it was business. She didn't ask what kind. It never occurred to her to suspect another woman. She knew Wendell, and she was right. His date for the evening was Peewee.

Wendell picked up Peewee in one of his liquor-hauling cars, another Hudson, and they headed for the drive-in, the Princess Theater. Maybe I'll take Mary tomorrow night, Wendell thought. There wasn't much chance of his seeing much of the picture tonight.

At the drive-in, Peewee told him to park in the last row, to the left, near the exit, then settled down happily with a bag of popcorn to watch the movie. Wendell wondered about his friend. How could anyone come up with the kind of impossible scheme that had been devised for tonight, then just sit back as if he didn't have a worry in the whole world?

Wendell had plenty of worries. There were the goddamn police watching the house almost every minute, forcing him to sneak around and wear disguises, forcing him to use a different car every time, forcing him to hide the cars in all kinds of places – and worst of all, forcing him to make direct deliveries. Direct deliveries were just too chancy. It got more nerve-wracking every day, and this idiot idea of Peewee's for tonight had to be about the worst.

Wendell tried to watch the movie. Ethel Waters filled the screen, a great big old woman. 'Hey, man,' he said, nudging Peewee, 'doesn't Ethel Waters remind you of my grandma?'

'Watch out, man,' Peewee complained. 'You're making me spill my popcorn.'

'That Ethel Waters is one hell of an actress.' Wendell just wanted to talk, to get rid of the nervousness that was building up inside him.

Ethel Waters was now giving Jeanne Craine advice. 'She's supposed to be Ethel Waters's granddaughter,' Peewee said. 'She look like a black girl to you?'

'No,' Wendell said. The whole story of the movie seemed to be about whether Jeanne Craine should be a black girl or not. Not many people get to make the choice, Wendell thought.

Unable to pay much mind to the picture, he looked around him at the rows of cars, all kinds of cars. Old jalopies full of whole families, the little kids running back and forth all the time to get some popcorn or go to the bathroom. Newer jalopies with couples, who seemed to be paying about as much attention to the movie as Wendell was. Pick-up trucks. Even a motorcycle or two. Could be a cop in any damn one of them, Wendell thought. Or an informer. He wished he were there with Mary and the baby, just taking in the movie like any lawful citizen.

'Shit, man, let's get going,' he said, nudging Peewee. 'Let's just get this whole crazy business over with. If there aren't any cops here tonight, we're the two luckiest people in the whole world.' He nudged Peewee again. 'Let's get going.'

'Wendell, you sure are a lousy date,' Peewee giggled. 'Won't even keep your hands to yourself and let me watch this picture.' He opened the door of the Hudson and reached across to knock on the door of the car parked to his right.

The occupant nodded and opened his doors, on both sides, then signalled the driver next to him, who opened his doors. The same thing happened with the next car, and the next, until there was a long pipeline of opened automobiles, along which Peewee began handing out the hootch. The jugs were passed from hand to hand between the parked cars as Wendell checked off his list. There were a couple of dozen small orders to be filled with the cooperation of the customers. If they could get away with this, Wendell thought, they could get away with anything.

'Okay, now,' said Peewee. 'That's about it. There should be three more for John Lee' – he passed out three more bottles – 'and three for Luther Reed.' Wendell checked off Luther Reed's order. 'Two for Sonny Clifton. And two for old Sweetwater Gallatin. That come out right, Wendell?' Peewee asked as he handed out the last bottles.

'That's right,' said Wendell, making the last check mark. 'It's all even. So let's haul ass.'

Peewee got back into the Hudson and slammed the door. Then a whole lot of doors slammed shut. It was hard to hear what Ethel Waters was saying, over the sounds of car doors slamming and engines being turned on. The back row of the drive-in began to empty out fast.

Peewee stared at the screen. 'Man, I wanted to see this movie,' he said. 'I don't know about you, Wendell. Seems like you've changed. Ever since you became a family man, you just want to run home early every night.'

'Jee-*zus*!' Wendell said. 'It's bad enough I let you talk me into this half-assed notion, but I am most sure as hell not going to hang around and watch the goddamn picture!'

As Wendell backed the Hudson out of its space, Peewee heaved his shoulders like a broken man. 'They're giving away a whole set of dishes after the show,' he said. 'I bet Mary sure would like those dishes.'

Wendell dropped Peewee off at Sweets' and left the Hudson in a different place from where he'd picked it up. Clean as a whistle, he walked home. He looked around to see if the cop was watching tonight, but for a change he didn't see anyone.

The next night he took Mary and the baby and his mother and his grandma to the drive-in to see Ethel Waters and Jeanne Craine in *Pinky*. They all liked it, even Wendell this time.

It was late when he turned the Lincoln into his own driveway. The baby was asleep in Mary's arms, and

Wendell noticed that the young cop in the patrol car across the street looked pretty tired, too. Where was *he* last night? he wondered. He helped Mary and the sleeping baby into the house, then waved goodnight to the cop before he shut off the porch light.

V

The new baby was another boy, and Wendell was pleased. So was Mary, and they decided to have just about as many babies as they could, and just as fast. Wendell, Jr., was tearing around now, and pretty soon, Wendell hoped, he'd be old enough to take to the races down at the Speedway.

But with all his family responsibilities, it looked as if it might take Wendell just a little bit longer to get out on that track himself. And he was letting up on hauling liquor for a while. The heat from the law was still on to an uncomfortable degree, and Wendell had money in the bank, so it might just be time for a temporary retirement. He could afford to coast for a while. Might just work up his garage business into a full-time thing and give up bootlegging for good, Wendell thought. He imagined himself walking into Sweets' and making his announcement. Christmas was near; he'd wait for New Year's Eve and tell everyone that he'd made a New Year's resolution. Wouldn't that stop old Peewee cold!

Mary gave him his best present the day before Christmas, when she told him she was pregnant again. Wendell hugged and kissed her. It was about time for a girl, they both agreed, a sister for Wendell, Jr., and little Frankie.

It was midnight before the tree was finally up and fixed just right. With all the packages around it, it looked as pretty as the pictures in magazines. Grandma Scott and Wendell's mother were coming over for dinner, and the whole Jones clan would be coming by later in the afternoon. Mary looked around the room and counted her blessings – except for one or two things, Wendell had given her a good life.

Christmas morning it took Wendell, Jr., about two

minutes to open all his presents. His favorite was a shiny red toy car. Watching him run it across the rug at great speed, Mary thought that he must have souped it up already. Thank God he hadn't thought about putting in two gearshifts yet, and if she had anything to say about it, such things would never be any of his concern. There'd be no bootlegging for their kids. Their children were going to go to college!

The telephone rang, and Wendell, who had just gone into the kitchen for a second cup of coffee, picked it up. 'Hello, Merry Christmas!' he said. Then his voice got too low to overhear and his expression became serious.

Mary heard Wendell hang up, and then he came into the living room. 'Honey,' he said, 'I'm truly sorry, but I'm going to have to make a quick run over to Lamont Cleveland's house.'

She was upset. 'A run? On Christmas Day?'

'I *am* sorry, baby,' he told her, 'but that was Simms on the phone and he's in one big bind. He promised old Cleveland some stuff for his big Christmas party, but he went and got sick. Simms, he could just hardly get out of bed. Now I know you don't like him, but if it wasn't for Simms we wouldn't have a lot of what we've got.'

Mary wasn't giving up easily. 'I don't think it's right, leaving your family at Christmas.'

'Come on and give me a hand, honey,' Wendell said.

She followed him back into the kitchen, but she didn't help as he disconnected the pipe from the stove to the chimney and began taking out bottles of moonshine. It was only when he started putting the bottles into shoeboxes that he brought in from the pantry that she took over. For a skilled mechanic, Wendell couldn't gift-wrap packages worth a damn.

'I'm glad to see you've got your Christmas spirit back, honey,' Wendell teased her as she wrapped.

'I just don't want you to be having your Christmas party with Sheriff Cotten,' Mary said. 'Don't you know it's broad daylight out there?'

'I'm going to take the cab,' he said. 'Now you know that the cops aren't going to figure that I'm carrying liquor in my own car, in broad daylight, on Christmas Day.'

He picked up the wrapped boxes, and Mary followed him out onto the front porch. He hugged her, then backed out the Lincoln. 'I'll be back in about an hour,' he called out as he turned into the street.

Wendell drove slowly through the quiet residential streets of black Danville, thinking of Mary and the boys and Christmas. He didn't even speed up when a patrol car pulled out of a side street and started to follow him. It was only when the cops – who happened to be Langer and Castle – hit the siren and the gas, both at the same time, that Wendell realized that they were after him.

The patrol car was alongside, trying to force him off the road. Shit, Wendell thought, it's almost as if they'd been waiting for me. He threw the Lincoln into reverse, wishing that this was one of his double-transmission cars, backed into an intersection, and got himself turned around. The cops made a wide U-turn and came after him again. If he couldn't outrun them or outfool them, maybe he could outnavigate them, he decided, and began a series of complicated maneuvers, turning sharply right and left, brakes squealing. The damned cops stayed right on him.

A hill was coming up. Wendell hit the accelerator, glanced in the rear-view mirror, and saw that the patrol car was already beginning to fall behind. It may turn out to be a merry Christmas after all, he thought. The Lincoln reached the crest of the hill. And as it began to descend on the other side, Wendell saw the children playing right out in the street, a lot of them. There was no side street and no alley, no place at all to turn, so he braked sharply and drove right up on the front lawn of Mr and Mrs Matthew Bibby, coming to a stop just before he hit the porch.

The Bibbys were old friends and clients. Hearing the commotion, Mrs Bibby came to the front window and pulled aside the curtain. Seeing that it was Wendell, she waved.

Wendell waved back as the kids started crowding around the car, curious about this man who had driven up on the Bibbys' lawn. No point in running, he thought. I'm in my own car, and the sign that says 'Scott's Taxi Service' couldn't be much bigger. But shit! It was finally happening. The Man was finally going to get his ass good.

Castle was the first of the cops to reach the Lincoln. 'Merry Christmas, Scott,' he said, looking real pleased with himself. Wendell got out of the car as Langer came up, eyeing the wrapped shoeboxes with interest. 'What's in there?'

'Christmas presents,' said Wendell.

'Christmas presents, my ass,' said Langer, taking a swing at Wendell with his nightstick. Wendell ducked to avoid the blow.

'Don't you be hitting on me,' he said. 'This is a federal case, and it's got nothing to do with you.'

Castle and Langer took him by the arms and escorted him to the patrol car. Langer seemed to be trying to break his arm, Wendell thought. Shit, the man must bear a grudge over that barbed-wire fence.

Langer did. 'Come on, Scott, why don't you try and escape?' he taunted. 'Get you a bullet right up your shiny black ass.'

Wendell did not resist as they shoved him into the back seat of the patrol car. On the way to the station he did some thinking. Goddamn it, he thought, they *were* waiting for me! And there was only one person who could have told them that he'd be running liquor that day. He should have realized it a long time ago – Henry Simms was just about the only person he knew in the trade who hadn't had some kind of trouble with the law. Simms was smart, but he wasn't that smart. He must have some other kind of a deal going for him.

Wendell thought about Mary and the kids. Some Christmas! Then he thought about Joe Robinson and almost smiled. Mary's old lawyer boyfriend was going to have to work on Christmas, too.

VI

'Merry Christmas, Scott,' said Sheriff Cotten. He grinned as he watched Wendell being fingerprinted. 'Well, we finally got you, and now we're going to throw the book at you.'

Langer emptied Wendell's pockets, and Castle started to put the change in an envelope. 'Leave me out a dime,' said Wendell. 'I get to make one phone call, if I'm not mistaken.'

Langer listened while Wendell spoke briefly to Robinson from the pay phone in the corridor. 'He'll be right down here,' said Wendell, hanging up, 'so don't you worry about finding me an extra comfortable cell.'

Sheriff Cotten grinned again as Wendell was led past him, on the way to the holding cells. Then he turned to the man sitting in the corner, wondering why in hell Billy Joe Byrnes wasn't at home with his family on Christmas Day. Still, Cotten was pleased enough about getting Scott in the slammer so that he wasn't going to make a fuss over Billy Joe's little piss-ant permit.

'Okay,' he said. 'Now, I understand that you want to drive those damn race cars up and down Main Street to drum up business.'

'Yeah,' said Billy Joe Byrnes. 'Get more people over to the Speedway, it's good business for everyone in Danville. I got some real good ideas for promoting the Speedway, and it just might turn out to be one of the biggest dirt tracks in the South.'

'You got your permit,' said Cotten. 'Come by tomorrow and get it in writing.'

But Billy Joe was curious about the scene he had just witnessed. 'Listen,' he asked, 'what was all that just now about? Who was that boy you-all seemed so happy to put away? He murder someone?'

Cotten smiled. 'No. That was that goddamn bootlegger Wendell Scott. We been after his ass for longer than I care to tell you. That boy's just about run my men ragged. Jesus! How he can drive!'

Billy Joe hitched his chair closer. 'You say he can out-drive your boys?'

Cotten was suddenly tired. 'Yeah,' he said. 'Scott's done pretty good against our boys. And to tell you the truth, we only got him now because – well, let's just say we got lucky. A little bird helped us out.'

Billy Joe was most definitely interested. 'Sheriff,' he said, 'can we go someplace private? Take a walk or something? I got an idea I want to talk to you about.'

Cotten gestured Billy Joe to his private office. 'Okay. But make it snappy. I got a lot of paperwork to do.'

The door of the private office was still closed when Joe Robinson finished talking to Wendell and headed for the pay telephone, wondering what he was going to tell Mary. The hell with it, he decided. Let one of Wendell's damn bootlegging friends do the dirty work! He called Peewee and gave him the basic information. Damn bootlegging and damn Wendell, Robinson thought as he hung up. Mary deserved something better than having her Christmas ruined by an irresponsible damn husband who couldn't keep his ass out of jail! Come to think of it, he himself, Joe Robinson, didn't much relish having to work on Christmas.

Robinson's back was turned, so he did not see Cotten and Billy Joe Byrnes emerge from the sheriff's private office. If he had seen them, he would have wondered why both men were smiling.

Peewee wasn't smiling as he hung up the receiver. So the Man got Wendell, he thought. And Wendell was out in his own car, doing a favor for old Henry Simms. He dialed Simm's number and let the phone ring for a good two minutes. Nobody home. Seemed as if maybe Simms wasn't too sick to go out after all. He started to dial Mary's number, then thought better of it. It wasn't good news he had for her, and it would probably be easier to tell her face to face.

Peewee drove slowly, allowing himself time to reflect. At the Scott house, he got reluctantly out of the car. He wasn't even on the porch before Mary opened the door. Momma Scott and Grandma Scott were right behind her with Grandma Scott holding Frankie. All three women looked worried.

'Merry Christmas, ladies,' said Peewee. He was smiling, but it didn't feel as if it fitted quite right.

Mary cut right through the smile. 'What's happened to Wendell?'

Peewee, still trying to hold the smile, followed her into the living room and flopped into an overstuffed chair that made him look even smaller. He looked at Wendell, Jr., playing under the tree. From the kitchen he caught the smell of the ham that was almost ready for Christmas dinner.

The women gathered around him. 'I said, what's happened to Wendell?' Mary repeated.

'What makes you think anything happened to your husband?' Peewee said.

Grandma Scott snapped at him. 'Peewee, if you're keeping anything from this girl, I'm going to stick you up the chimney and set that cute little behind of yours on fire!'

Peewee sagged. His smile and bravado both vanished. 'Cops got Wendell,' he said. 'They're holding him down at the station house, waiting for the Federal men to come and get him.'

Mary grabbed the back of a chair, so hard that her fingers turned white. 'Why hasn't he called?' she said.

'He only got one call,' Peewee said. 'He called Joe Robinson, and Robinson called me, told me to come over and stay with you-all until we hear from him.'

Mary turned to Momma Scott. 'My God, Momma, what are we going to do?' she cried. Grandma Scott put Frankie down and settled Mary on the sofa.

'I don't know,' Mary sobbed as the two women tried to soothe her. 'I just don't know. I – well, I used to sometimes wish that they *would* catch him . . . '

Peewee couldn't believe his ears.

'Not to put him in jail or anything,' Mary went on, 'but just to kind of give him a scare, just scare him enough so that he'd stop. I can't take much more of this, I just can't take it. Driving that cab all day, then sneaking off every night to haul liquor! I just don't know what I'm going to do!'

Peewee was getting a pretty good idea of what to do. He looked at the festive tree, and smelled the ham, and watched Wendell, Jr., and Frankie playing on the floor. Then he looked again at the women. It was Henry Simms that was responsible for Mary's crying and taking on like that. It was bad enough that Wendell was in jail, but seeing Mary cry was even worse.

Momma Scott gave him a hard look. 'What are you muttering to yourself like that for?' she asked. 'Peewee, you seem like you know more about this than you're letting on. What is it?'

'Nothing, Mrs Scott.' Peewee stood up. 'It's just that I've got me a pretty good notion of why Wendell got caught. Now, if you ladies can excuse me and be all right by yourselves until lawyer Robinson comes, I have a little business to transact.'

Mary looked up at him. 'Peewee,' she said, 'don't *you* go getting yourself in any trouble.'

Peewee paused with his hand on the doorknob. 'Don't you worry about me and trouble,' he said. 'I ain't *getting* – I'm *giving*!'

VII

By New Year's Eve, Peewee had everything in order.

Sweets' was jammed when he walked in that night. The parking lot was full, and the road was lined with parked cars in both directions. Peewee wondered how all those people were going to get into Sweets', but he didn't care. He had a reservation, and a date with Alma and Luanne and Henry Simms.

At the bar, the bartender gave Peewee a glass of whiskey, compliments of the house, and he stood for a moment under the big 'Happy New Year' banners, looking around for his party. Where the hell were they? What with the smoke and the people crowding the dance floor, it was hard to tell. He spotted them across the room and snaked his way over, banging into chairs and tables and it seemed like about everyone in the county.

He sat down between Alma and Luanne, giving each of them a kiss on the cheek. He set his glass in front of him, but did not take a drink – New Year's Eve or not, tonight wasn't for fun. Simms was seated across the table. The girls had gotten him drinking early, as Peewee had told them to, and he looked pretty far gone. Simms's eyes were red, and Peewee wondered how the man could see, his eyelids looked so heavy.

Simms had been telling a story, and he went on with it. 'Anyway,' he said, 'this old boy is so drunk that after he loses the bolt down inside the engine block, he decides not to take the head off. So what do you think he does?'

Peewee was finding it hard to think over the noise of the jukebox. And he sure as hell wasn't thinking about Simms's story.

'What do you think he does?' Simms was glowering.

Peewee let it go by, and the girls, taking their cue from him, looked disinterested. Luanne signalled for another round of drinks, while Alma leaned over to the table to her right, and asked a stranger for a light, letting him get a good look at her breasts.

Simms was beginning to look dangerous and Peewee decided that an answer might be required. 'I pass,' he said.

Alma giggled, but stopped when Simms brought his fist down on the table. 'I'll tell you what he does!' Simms said. 'What this turkey does is, he wraps a chain hoist around the whole goddamn car and turns it upside down, trying to shake the bolt out.' He was laughing so hard that he could hardly speak. 'Don't that beat all?' he spluttered.

Peewee looked blank, but Simms was still laughing when the fresh drinks arrived. Alma pushed a glass toward Peewee, but he ignored it as he had the first one, which still stood before him on the table.

Simms calmed down, and Luanne asked, 'Did it come out?'

'What?'

'Did the bolt come out?' Luanne persevered.

'Hell, I don't know if the damned bolt came out or not,' Simms said. 'Whole point of the story is turning the car upside down! Ain't it a bitch?' He shook with laughter again.

Peewee looked around the room. He didn't really expect to recognize the parties he was looking for. And he really didn't need to – with any luck he'd never see them again.

Simms whispered something in Luanne's ear. Over his shoulder, the girl looked at Peewee, who checked his watch and nodded.

'Okay, sugar,' Luanne said to Simms. 'You and me are going to get out of here right away. Won't even stay around to see the New Year in. We've got better things to do!'

She should have giggled right there, but she didn't.

'But listen, baby,' Luanne went on, 'I have to go to the powder room. It'll only take one minute, but don't you wait for me. Why don't you go out and warm up the car – you know I can't stand being cold. Then I'll come right on out to the parking lot and we can start the New Year *right*.'

'Now you're talking, honey,' Simms said. 'And don't

you worry. I have no intention at all of letting you get cold. Don't be long.' He got out his wallet and tried to place some bills on the table.

Peewee pushed his hand away. 'Put that away. Tonight's on me.'

Simms stared.

'You heard me,' said Peewee. 'Your money's no good in here tonight. I'm taking care of everything.'

Simms mumbled something and began to work his way, somewhat unsteadily, toward the door. Luanne was suddenly all business as she gathered her things together, and hightailed it for the back door. Before she went out, she nodded to two men seated near the door to the powder room. Peewee saw the nod, but he didn't stand or even crane his neck to see the two men. It was enough just to know that they were there and had gotten Luanne's high sign.

One of the two men dropped a twenty-dollar bill on the table, and they both stood up. It was a lot of money, considering that they hadn't been drinking much of anything, but they didn't wait for change. They walked swiftly toward the front door, maneuvering through the crowd with the ease of quarterbacks. They were big men, but that was all that Peewee was able to make out as they followed Simms out the door. They didn't stop to get their coats and hats, if they'd ever had any.

Peewee and Alma sat in silence at their table.

In the parking lot, Simms got into his car and turned on the ignition and the heater, wanting it nice and warm for Luanne. Then he fiddled with the radio. Between the heater and the radio, he didn't hear the two men approach. By the time he realized they were there, it was too late to reach under the dashboard for his revolver. The bullets came through the front and side windows, shattering the glass, and Henry Simms was blown away.

The two men got into their own car and drove out of Sweets' parking lot. The sound of the shots had been drowned by the sounds of the New Year's crowd in Sweets', and it was some time before someone found Simms and called the cops.

It was only when he heard the police sirens that Peewee relaxed and took his first drink of the evening.

VIII

Wendell's trial came in early March in the Fifth District Court of the State of Virginia, Judge Clark Van Buren presiding.

Joe Robinson had waived trial by jury, thinking that he'd have a better chance of getting his client off with a judge alone. Still, things didn't look too good, since Wendell was just plain guilty as hell.

In the courtroom, the morning the trial was to begin, Robinson arranged an assortment of papers in neat piles on the long table at which he and Wendell were seated. For a while, the scratching of his pencil on his notepad was the only sound in the room.

Wendell fidgeted as he waited, but settled down a little after Mary, his mother, and his grandma entered the court. Then he began to fidget again as he watched the prosecuting attorney, a cocky little lawyer who was bucking for state attorney general. Everybody knew that, and Wendell didn't want to provide him with another stepping-stone to higher office.

Peewee arrived just in time to sit down beside Mary before the county clerk called out, 'All rise.' Judge Van Buren came into court through a side door and took his place on the bench. He yawned slightly as he banged the gavel. Court was called to order.

Wendell didn't listen to the reading of the charges. He knew all too well what they were. Leaning over to Robinson, he asked, 'Is that the same Judge Van Buren that gave Naddy Wobass five years?' Robinson nodded. Oh, shit, thought Wendell, what's to make this judge give *me* any less? The man's got it in for bootleggers. 'Man,' he said to Robinson, 'this cat's going to throw the book at me.'

'Don't worry,' said Robinson, 'we have a good story.' Privately, he wondered just how good it really was.

Judge Van Buren drank a large glass of water before he finally got down to the case. 'Will the defendant please rise and face the bench,' he said. 'Wendell Scott, having heard the charges against you, and with full knowledge of such charges, how say you: guilty or not guilty?'

Wendell stood and faced the bench, wanting to run, and for a second he couldn't remember how he did say. He looked at Robinson, who nodded encouragingly. 'Not guilty,' said Wendell. His knees collapsed beneath him, and he sat down again. Nobody tried to make him get back up.

'The defendant pleads not guilty,' Judge Van Buren confirmed. He addressed the prosecuting attorney. 'Mr Wright,' he said, 'will you kindly present your opening statement?'

Everything about Wright set Wendell's teeth on edge. An uppity little bastard, he thought.

Wright smiled ingratiatingly at the bench. 'Your Honor,' he began, 'we shall prove here today that the defendant, Wendell Scott, a known bootlegger – '

Joe Robinson was out of his chair like a rocket. 'Objection!' he shouted. 'He can't call my client a bootlegger!'

'Objection sustained,' said Judge Van Buren. 'Please confine yourself to the facts, Mr Wright.' He poured himself another glass of water, and Wendell began to wonder if what looked like water might not really be white lightning.

Attorney Wright called Officer Langer to the stand. 'Officer Langer,' said Wright, 'will you tell the court briefly what happened on the afternoon of last December twenty-fifth?'

'Yes, sir,' said Langer. 'Officer Castle and myself, we was cruising along Hill Road, when we spied the defendant, Wendell Scott, rushing into his car just in front of us. Since the defendant is known for bootlegging, we decided just to have a little look-see . . .'

'Objection,' Robinson shouted.

'Sustained,' said Judge Van Buren. 'Go on, Officer Langer.'

'Well, Your Honor,' said Langer, 'when we spied the

defendant, we went after him. On seeing us approaching, he speeded up well past the legal limit – '

Robinson was on his feet for the third time. 'Objection!' he said. 'My client has not been charged with speeding, and unless he was clocked in the manner prescribed by law – '

'Sustained,' said Judge Van Buren. 'And Mr Robinson, will you please stop jumping around so much? You're making me nervous. Mr Wright, please ask the witness to rephrase his testimony.'

Wright asked Langer to rephrase his statement, and Langer tried. 'Well, when Scott saw us, he lit out like a cat with its tail on fire. We followed, and the next thing we knew, he had spun out and driven clean up onto the porch of 578 Mill Road. Home of a family named Bibby. We apprehended the defendant on the lawn of the aforementioned Bibby family, and upon searching his car found six bottles of illicit and contraband whiskey.'

'May we please have the whiskey placed in evidence?' Wright asked, and an attendant set the shoeboxes on the table, half of them still gaily wrapped for Christmas.

'Your Honor, the people place this whiskey in evidence as Exhibit Number One,' Wright said. The judge was having another drink of water or whatever the hell it was. Wendell decided that he really didn't care. He just wanted this trial to be over with.

'And then,' Wright asked Langer, 'what did you do?'

'Then Officer Castle and myself took the defendant to the station for booking. And we had him held there until we could turn him over to the Federal authorities for transportation of contraband whiskey.'

The rage suddenly swelled up in Langer. He'd taken enough from that goddamn Scott, and now he was going to have his say. Ignoring Wright's thanks and permission to leave the witness stand, he turned to the judge.

'Your Honor,' Langer burst out, 'this man Scott's the biggest bootlegger in Danville! Why, everybody knows it, but you can't catch him at it! He's already destroyed five-six of our police cars, must have cost the city thousands of dollars – '

He stopped as Judge Van Buren pounded his gavel. Joe Robinson was shouting his fifth or sixth 'Objection!'

and some of the spectators were beginning to titter, especially Peewee. The judge gave one last good whack and called for order.

'Officer Langer,' he said, 'one more outburst like that, and I'll hold you in contempt of court. And Mr Robinson, for God's sake, will you *please* sit down?'

Wendell had to turn away to keep from laughing. As he did so, he caught Mary's eye and that set her off. A second more and the whole back row of the courtroom – Mary, Peewee, Momma Scott, and Grandma Scott – was shaking with laughter. Momma Scott finally got them rounded up and out of the courtroom after a glare from Judge Van Buren brought her momentarily to her senses.

'Court is recessed until after lunch,' the judge announced.

Billy Joe Byrnes, sitting up front, wondered just what in hell all the commotion in the back of the courtroom had been about. He had been studying Wendell so hard that he had not turned to look.

IX

None of the women felt like eating, and Peewee wanted only a drink. He sipped at it as they all sat around the Scotts' living room, waiting for news. There had been general agreement that they had better not go back to the courthouse.

Mary sat with her hands folded over her stomach, the way pregnant women do, even though she wasn't really beginning to show yet. 'Momma,' she said to Mrs Scott, 'so help me God, if Wendell gets out of this, I swear I'm not ever going to let him carry one more ounce of liquor.'

Grandma Scott answered her. 'Child, don't be saying things that you might be regretful of. Wendell's a good provider. He's a little wild now, but then so was his daddy. And you know that you can't make a man do what you want by telling him he's got to do it. Sooner or later he'll steady down, and then he'll think it was all his own idea.'

Peewee's eyes opened wide. He'd never heard women plotting like this before. Doesn't apply to me, Peewee thought. They're not my family. But hell, they were Wendell's, and it was just about the same thing.

Frankie woke up from his nap and began yelling, so Mary went off to get him before Wendell, Jr., woke up, too. She had just returned with the baby when Wendell burst into the room. Handing Frankie to Grandma Scott, she ran to her husband.

'Hoooo-eeeey!' Wendell yelled. 'Probation! Honey, I got off with probation!' His hug lifted Mary clear of the floor. Joe Robinson was right behind him, and Momma Scott gave him a big hug, since she couldn't get to Wendell just that minute.

Robinson was excited, too. 'Probation!' he yelled. 'That old bastard gave him three years' probation! Can you beat that?' He danced around with Momma Scott. Peewee pounded everyone on the back.

Wendell and Joe Robinson were both talking fast and telling the same thing, about what had happened after Judge Van Buren had dismissed the court and called them and prosecutor Wright into his private chambers.

'Hey, man, what kind of story you give him?' Peewee asked. 'We all know you was guilty as hell!'

Grandma Scott scowled at him. She knew as well as anyone that Wendell was guilty as hell, but he didn't have to come right out and say it like that.

'I told him I was going out to start somebody's car.' Wendell stood with his arm around Mary, who didn't care what he'd told Judge Van Buren or anyone else, just as long as he was home. 'I had my tools in the trunk to prove it. Told him I never thought I was doing anything illegal just carrying Christmas presents. Told him a man asked me to do him a favor and drop them off at his house.'

'And he bought that?' asked Peewee.

'Hell, no, he didn't buy it,' said Joe Robinson. 'How could he have?'

'He said "Guilty as charged." ' Wendell was now imitating Judge Van Buren's bored voice. 'But then he gave me probation! I'm free as a bird, unless they catch me again! And it took them a long time to catch me the first time!'

Mary decided that she and Wendell were going to have a good serious talk just as soon as the others cleared out. Now here was Joe Robinson – Joe Robinson, of all people – saying 'How about a drink?' She hadn't known he even touched the stuff.

'I got me some of the best moonshine made in this entire county,' Robinson said, opening his briefcase and pulling out a pint bottle.

Lawyer Robinson, thought Wendell, walking right into that courthouse with a pint of illegal hootch right under the judge's nose. Well, I'll be damned! Looked like it took more than a fancy law degree from up north to spoil a man's taste. Wendell wondered what old man Jones would think if he could see Robinson now.

Peewee came out of the kitchen with a load of glasses,

which Robinson began filling all around. Wendell had time for just a sip of his before he heard the knock at the door. Handing his glass to Peewee, he went to see who it was.

It was Sheriff Cotten and Billy Joe Byrnes. It took Wendell a second or two to recognize Byrnes as the man who had been sitting in the back of the courtroom that morning. What did these two want with him now? Wendell glanced nervously into the room behind him, but the bottle and glasses of illegal liquor had disappeared. Must have hid everything in the sofa, he thought.

In the living room, Billy Joe stuck out his hand and said, 'Howdy! I'm Billy Joe Byrnes. Glad to make your acquaintance.'

Wendell shook his hand, but he was looking at Cotten.

'Wendell,' said Cotten, 'this is not an official visit. If you can spare a few minutes, I think you might be interested in what Mr Byrnes has to say.'

Billy Joe was introducing himself all over the room, but not till the fourth time did Wendell actually hear what he was saying. '... Billy Joe Byrnes. Maybe you-all have heard of me? I own the race track here in town.'

'You own the raceway?' Wendell said. 'The Danville Speedway?'

'Wendell,' Cotten said, 'could you and me and Billy Joe have us a little private conversation?'

'Don't see why not,' said Wendell. He led them into the kitchen and closed the door. What in hell was happening? He leaned against the sink, waiting.

Billy Joe Byrnes spoke right up. 'Wendell, being as I don't like to beat around the bush, I'll come right to the point. My friend here, Sheriff Cotten – who I think you know – tells me that you just got off with three years' probation. Well, I think that's mighty fine. But my friend here, Sheriff Cotten, also tells me that next time you ain't going to get off so easy, so –'

'That's damn-all right, Wendell,' the sheriff interrupted. 'What Billy Joe's trying to say is that if I catch you moving so much as a pint of moon, I'll have your ass so hard ... well, do I make myself clear?' His voice was not angry; he was just stating the rules.

'You come all the way out here to tell me that?' said Wendell.

'Now, hold on there, you two, hold on,' Billy Joe Byrnes said. 'Let's all be friends. Now, Wendell, I got me a proposition to make you, but before I do, there's one real important thing I want you to know. That wasn't just luck that got you off with three years' probation. Nor was it your smart lawyer Robinson. When you're looking for someone to thank, you can just look around you right here. It was me and Cotten did it.'

Wendell looked hard at the two men, studying their faces. They didn't look like they were lying, but what was in it for them? He'd have thought Cotten would want him locked up for a hundred years rather than out on probation. Just then Billy Joe Byrnes came to the point.

'Wendell, how'd you like to drive a stock car for me over at the Speedway?'

Wendell couldn't believe that he was hearing right. 'Drive a stock car??' he said. For one wild split second, it looked as if his dream might be coming true. But then reality took over. This man was having some kind of joke on him, and it wasn't funny.

'No black man's allowed to race stock cars,' he said.

'Nothing says he can't,' said Billy Joe. 'Thing is, no colored man knows *how* to race stock cars, so far as I know. But I know lots of folks here in town will pay good money to see some of you people race some of my drivers.'

'Is that why you're here?' Wendell still wasn't sure that he was getting it just right. 'You want me to race a stock car over at the Speedway?'

'That's right,' said Billy Joe. 'I went to see the sheriff, and I told him I needed some colored boys to race cars, and he said "I don't know but one – his name is Scott, and you're welcome to him." That's what the man said, that you were the best. What about it? Think you can handle it?'

Wendell wanted to shout, but he managed to keep his voice down. 'Sure I can handle it,' he said calmly. 'Who else you got?'

'Nobody, boy,' Billy Joe replied. 'You're it. But I got me about a dozen of my best white drivers who are real eager to take you on.'

Jee-zus! thought Wendell, I'll just bet they are. Trying to make out that he'd been wheeling and dealing with raceway promoters all his life, he asked, 'What's in it for me?'

'If you win,' said Billy Joe, '*if* you win, you get the whole purse, and that's a pretty good pile of money.' He was suddenly brisk and businesslike. 'Well, what do you say? I ain't got all day.'

'Where do I get me a race car?' Wendell asked.

Billy Joe's face had turned hard. He was no longer just passing through to do a few favors. He had got him a colored driver – that much was clear from Wendell's face – and now that colored driver could shift for himself.

'That's *your* problem,' he said. 'You just be down at the Speedway by one o'clock Sunday. You hear? And you ain't going to let me down, are you boy? Why, I might even put your name in the papers.'

'I'll be there,' said Wendell.

Billy Joe was all smiles again. 'Well,' he said, 'seems like this calls for a drink.'

Damned if it doesn't, thought Wendell. He turned and opened the cabinet under the sink. Sheriff Cotten came up behind him, fast, and peered over his shoulder. This was the first opportunity the sheriff had had to get an actual look at Wendell Scott's stash.

Wendell looked back over his shoulder and smiled.

'Just trying to see where you keep the stuff,' said Cotten, feeling a little bit silly. 'Doesn't hurt to try.'

'Just keep on trying,' said Wendell, as he found what he was looking for and stood up, holding a nice legal bottle of Canadian Club. The three of them each had a snort of the whiskey. Then Wendell led them out of the kitchen door and around the house to where they had left their car. Billy Joe shook hands with Wendell again, but Sheriff Cotten just nodded. Wendell watched them drive away, then turned and burst back into the living room.

'Going to drive at the Speedway!' he shouted.

It was no news to his family and friends, since Peewee had been listening at the kitchen door and had passed on the information. Everyone applauded, and there was much hugging and kissing of Wendell. The glasses of moonshine appeared again, and in response to Peewee's toast – 'To the fastest-assed cat of them all!' – even Mary had a little sip.

There were more toasts, and Wendell entertained with an imitation of Billy Joe Byrnes. 'No colored man knows *how* to race stock cars, so far as I know,' he mimicked. Then he added a comment of his own. 'Shee-it!'

But in the middle of the merriment his face grew solemn, and he turned to Grandma Scott. 'Grandma,' he said, 'you remember the night I got home from the army? Remember how I told you I was going to win races all over the country? Well, let me tell you now, it looks like I just might be able to do that very thing.'

It seemed to Grandma Scott that there was a good chance that the white drivers down at the Speedway would probably try to kill this wild boy. But seeing the elation on Wendell's face, she said only, 'It looks like you might do just that. Yes, it does look like you might.'

X

Sunday was upon him almost before Wendell was ready for it. He'd spent the last four days fixing up one of his liquor cars, making it the closest thing to a stock car that he knew how. He'd chosen an old Plymouth, stripped it as much as possible, installed a homemade bucket seat, chained the doors so they wouldn't fly open, and tuned the motor fine as could be.

The last thing to do was paint a number on the door with fast-drying enamel, and he was doing that when Peewee and Robinson came over to the house. Peewee was going to take Mary and the babies to the race; Robinson would pick up Momma and Grandma Scott. Wendell, looking up from his work, waved a greeting to both of them. 'Well, what do you think of it?'

Peewee approached the Plymouth. 'Sure is pretty.' He looked worried. 'Think it'll run like those other cars, Wendell? I mean, they're special built.'

Wendell laughed. 'This one is sure as hell special built, Peewee. It's never let me down hauling moonshine. You ought to know that better than almost anyone else, little man.'

Robinson was inspecting the inside of the car. 'I don't know,' he said. 'I looked into one of those stock cars once, and it didn't look all that much different from this one. But it had a whole lot of metal bars going every which way inside it. It seemed like it might be a little sturdier than this.'

Mary came out in the yard just in time to catch these last words. Shit, thought Wendell, that's all she needs to hear.

'Well, it looks like you're about finished,' Mary said as Wendell backed away from the numbered door and moved around to the other side. Then she added what she didn't have to say, realizing that a second too late. 'They're going to give you a rough time out there.'

'Tell me something new,' Wendell snarled. He could have bitten off his tongue, talking to Mary like that.

'I know you want to do this,' she said. 'And I know you have to do this. But I wish you wouldn't.'

'I'm no fool,' Wendell said. 'Nothing I can't handle is going to happen to me.'

'It's going to be only you against all of them,' Mary persisted.

'Like I said . . . ' His words trailed off. He'd better just stop talking and save up his meanness for the race, he thought. If Mary was right, and he knew she was, he'd need all of it. 'Honey,' he said calmly, 'why don't you offer Peewee and Joe some coffee?'

Robinson decided he'd have his coffee in the kitchen with Mary, but Peewee elected to stay out and help Wendell. Squinting critically at the car, he said, 'Thirty-four. How come you chose that number?'

For a minute Wendell thought it was just a number he'd always liked, for no particular reason. Then he remembered. 'Once,' he told Peewee, 'when I was just a little boy, my daddy gave me a picture of a racer. And it was number thirty-four, so I guess that's why.'

Peewee was being deliberately cheerful, but he was as concerned as Mary was. 'Well,' he said, 'it looks real good, and if this racing business doesn't work out, you've still got yourself a good bootlegging car. Of course, I guess you'd have to take the numbers off it.'

Wendell finished the painting and straightened up. 'Peewee,' he said, 'I'll tell you this. With me on probation, and the Man all around, it may be that racing cars is going to be a lot safer than hauling moonshine.'

'You could be right,' Peewee said, 'but ever since Simms got his, the Man isn't going to find it as easy to ambush everybody.' He looked oddly proud of himself.

'Yeah,' said Wendell. 'How about that, old Simms turning folk in just to keep his own ass out of jail. I reckon he'd have turned his own mother in, if he'd had one.'

'Sure,' Peewee said. 'But hell, don't mind Simms now. Fire her up, and let's see how she sounds.'

Wendell climbed into the Plymouth through the window on the driver's side and started the engine. Without any muffler, it made a wonderful racket. Peewee and he both laughed, and after he gunned it three or four times, Mary and Joe Robinson came out of the house to admire all the commotion. Wendell smiled at Mary, beginning to feel good again. Whatever happened today, it was going to be a start. This afternoon he would be getting at least a little bit of his dream.

'You-all better get going,' he said to his audience as he cut the motor. 'You want to get you seats right up front in the grandstand, and I'll bet that with me driving today, the colored stands are going to be crammed full.'

Mary kissed him through the window, then went to get the kids. Peewee and Robinson went with her. Nobody wished Wendell luck out loud. Nobody needed to.

Wendell checked out his gear again, then headed for Main Street to join the parade of cars on the way to the Speedway. The other race cars were being towed, their drivers riding along in fancy cars, waving to the crowds, while their pit crews took care of business. Wendell didn't have a tow car or a pit crew, or any of the finery that the white drivers had. He just had his hastily built racer. But that, he figured, was damn well enough.

He watched some of the other cars pass, waiting until he thought it was about the end of the line. Then, all by himself, driving his racer, he joined in. Main Street and then McGill Avenue, which led right to the Speedway, were lined with people. Most of them knew every driver, every number, and every make of car that was going to be in the race. Wendell stood out like a sore thumb, and he knew it. The jeers and catcalls were about what he'd expected – hell, dirt-track racing didn't always attract exactly the nicest part of the white population, either from Danville or from the country. In fact, the 'best' families in town, the richest ones, just tried to pretend that the Danville Speedway wasn't there.

The crowd grew even thicker as Wendell got closer to the Speedway itself. It was mostly families, he noticed – men carrying picnic baskets, women carrying babies and trying to keep the older kids from running out into the traffic. There were quite a few 'good old boys', too, some of them already slugging out of bottles hidden in brown paper bags. They were the ones who could get ugly, he thought, then changed his mind as a pretty young matron yelled at him. 'Hey, nigger! Get back to the cotton fields!'

Wendell drove on around the stadium, past the main entrance, and past the sign that said 'Colored Section'. There was quite a crowd here, too. It looked as if every black man, woman, and child in Danville had turned out. At the front of the line waiting to get in, Wendell saw his family. Looked like Grandma Scott was the very first one. And she'd get in first, too – there wasn't anyone who could push his way past that big old lady. The whole line cheered as he went past, and Wendell felt proud. He grinned when he noticed the sign that said 'Admission Two Dollars'. By damn, old Billy Joe really was counting on him as a draw. The price of admission had been upped – used to be only a dollar-fifty, and that no later than last Sunday.

Wendell turned off into the Speedway's drivers' entrance. As he drove up the ramp, headed for the infield, a security guard stepped in front of him, stuck out his arm like a traffic cop, and told him to stop.

'Hey, boy,' said the guard, 'just where do you think you're going?'

Shit, thought Wendell, this son of a bitch knows damn well where I'm going. There is exactly one black driver in this race today, and the news has been all over town, and if this isn't a race car I don't know what it is! He kept his temper long enough to say, 'I'm Wendell Scott. And I'm racing here today. And with your kind permission, I'll just drive right on in.'

Saying nothing, the guard just walked around the car, checking the license plate, checking the interior – like he was some kind of real cop, looking for moonshine. Wendell had half a mind to drive right over the nosey bastard, but this was his day to race, and no dumb guard was going to spoil it for him.

Billy Joe Byrnes, watching the scene, figured that it had gone on long enough. He walked over to the guard and put a hand on his arm. 'That's okay, Charlie,' he said. 'He's with me. This here's Wendell Scott.'

'Excuse me, *Mister* Scott,' the guard said. 'I plumb didn't recognize you.'

Like shit you didn't, thought Wendell. But at least the guard had stood aside and was now waving him through.

Billy Joe pointed down the ramp to the infield, where a freshly-painted sign designated a privy as the 'Colored Toilet'. I guess that's why the price of admission had gone up fifty cents a head, Wendell thought. 'Go right in, Wendell,' Billy Joe said. 'You can change in there.'

Wendell wondered what the hell he was supposed to change into. He was going to drive in just what he had on – an old pair of cotton pants, a khaki shirt, work shoes. He was damned lucky to have the car fixed up in time for this event; he sure hadn't wasted any effort on a fancy uniform.

He drove onto the infield, parked in front of the new privy, and got out. The spectators in the black section yelled their heads off.

XI

Watching Wendell drive onto the infield, Billy Joe worried a little. He found it hard to credit his eyes. Here was this boy who had a reputation as one of the fastest, meanest, wildest drivers on God's green earth, but he didn't look as if he knew the first thing about racing. Teach me to hire hicks, Billy Joe thought. Where was Scott's pit crew? What the hell kind of a car did he call that? Billy Joe suppressed a shudder as he looked at Number Thirty-Four's tires. He was probably sending Scott to a sure death. Then he brightened up. The sure death of a new driver was what this crowd had come to see, for the most part. Even Sheriff Cotten, normally a kindly man, had suggested that if the white drivers didn't run Wendell right off the track, Billy Joe could count on having the Speedway torn right down. And Scott most surely did bring the colored crowd. The colored grandstand was full to overflowing. Billy Joe watched Wendell enter the new colored toilet.

Wendell adjusted his helmet before the already cracked mirror. He might not have a fancy uniform, but by God, he did have a helmet. It might be a little older than the crash helmets the other drivers were wearing – it was, in fact, his old high-school football helmet – but it would give some protection. And Wendell knew that he was going to need protection. He'd seen most of these dudes drive before, and the least mean among them could put a snake to shame. They were going to bang him around as much as they could. Shit, they banged each other around, even though some of them had to be friends, the way they raced together and drank beer together and cut up together. From what he'd heard, most of these boys were outlaws of a sort that made some of his bootlegging acquaintances seem downright tame. The meanest of the white drivers, by all reports, was a cat called Beau Welles. Wendell knew what Welles looked like and what car he'd be driving. That information might just make it a little easier to stay in one piece.

Wild cheers came again from the colored section of the grandstand as Wendell came out of the toilet and got back into the Plymouth. About a dozen cars were parked at the starting line, and he parked behind the last of them. He sat in the car, trying not to look at the knot of white drivers standing in the infield, swapping jokes. He didn't have to be a mind reader to know that some of the jokes must be about him. A few of the white boys looked at him, then looked away.

Wendell spotted Beau Welles talking to another driver, a dude named Bubba White, and Welles caught him looking.

'Hey, Bubba,' Welles said, ostensibly to White, but loud enough for Wendell to hear. 'Do you see what I see? Mr Byrnes said we was going to be racing some colored gentlemen, but this here's just ridiculous.' Then he addressed Wendell directly. 'Hey, boy, where'd you get that pretty hat?'

Wendell looked straight ahead and said nothing. Hell, he hadn't come here to socialize! Some of the other drivers drifted over to get a look at him and his car, but he continued to stare into space.

'Hey, boy, you better watch it,' Bubba White said flatly. 'You going to get yourself killed this afternoon.'

A track official came around with a hat, and the other drivers drew numbers from it. When he reached Wendell, there was just one slip of paper left to take. Wendell looked at it – number twelve.

The official smiled. 'Well, boy,' he said, 'I guess you just stay lined up right where you are. You start last.'

The other drivers began jockeying their cars into starting position. Billy Joe walked over to Wendell and put his head through the car window to give some last-minute instructions. 'Now, boy, when the green flag is waved, you take off 'round the track. You get it?'

Shit, yes, I get it, thought Wendell. Sweet Jesus, the

man must think he'd never seen a race in his life, instead of sitting in the grandstand about every Sunday.

'It's going to be twenty-five laps,' Billy Joe went on, 'and a lap is one time around the track.'

This dude's missed out on his calling in life, Wendell thought. He shouldn't be running a racetrack, he should be teaching idiot children. I bet he'd be real good at it. He began to drum his fingers on the steering wheel impatiently.

Billy Joe noticed the drumming. 'And don't be nervous, boy,' he said. 'Now, if you've got to change tires or anything, you pull off into the infield there and into the pits. Yellow flag means caution, red flag means stop, white flag means one lap to go. And the checker means the race is over. Got that?'

Yes! I got it! Wendell silently screamed. But as far as Billy Joe could tell, he just nodded.

'Good,' said Billy Joe. 'Now who's your mechanic? Who's going to do your pit work?'

'Been doing it myself up to now,' Wendell said. 'I don't see any reason to change.'

Billy Joe walked away shaking his head. It was all right that Wendell was going to lose, but he didn't really want to see him killed. He was good for business. But he was clearly crazy as a loon. Hell, Billy Joe thought, you had to be crazy to want to drive a stock car, anyhow. He reached the infield and nodded to the starter to signal the parade lap.

At the end of the procession once again, Wendell looked into the colored grandstand. There were his family, his friends, and his neighbors, all yelling their lungs out for him. Man, he thought, whatever happens, this has got to be just about the greatest day of my life! This is really what it's all about.

The green flag fell, and the race was on.

During the first lap, Wendell stuck in last place, feeling nervous. Then he began to get the feel of the car and opened up. During the next five laps he overtook one car after another. His years of racing through the hills were standing him in good stead; his instincts held true on gauging the turns, allowing him to ease up on the gas pedal at the last possible second, until he was into the turn and then bringing his foot to the floorboard again. And he didn't mind taking the high groove on the turns. He'd been in rougher situations than high groove.

By the eighth lap Wendell was in fifth place. He was about even with Bubba White when he felt the seat begin to come loose under him. He dropped back a little as he adjusted himself to hold on with his arm out over the door, so he could keep himself steady. Some of the other cars had been banging into his Plymouth pretty hard, trying to spin him out, and the banging was beginning to show. The chained door was rattling, but Wendell hung on in fifth position, and then the gear selector started jumping in and out. Goddamn, he thought, what else can go wrong? At that moment, the accelerator pedal fell off. With five laps to go, he had only the hand throttle!

Back in seventh place, Beau Welles was madder than hell. It was an insult to be on the track with a nigger, it was an insult to be on the track with a car like that homegrown Plymouth, and it was the worst insult of all to be *behind* a nigger in a homegrown Plymouth! Why doesn't the black bastard spin out? Welles wondered. What's keeping that goddamn wreck on the track? He's making monkeys out of all of us! It was just about time to teach the nigger a lesson, Welles decided, get his black ass off the track for good.

Wendell was coming off a turn, riding the low groove, when Welles came off the high side and headed right for him. Wendell braked hard. Welles shot past him and hit Bubba White alongside, pushing him into the infield and out of the race. Welles bounced back onto the track, causing Wendell to brake again.

Wendell realized that he wasn't going to regain much speed with his disintegrating car. Other drivers began to pass him, and now the white flag was out. He worked the Plymouth hard, but without much luck. When the checkered flag dropped, he was in eighth place. What the hell, he'd run the race and finished! And from the very beginning, the odds had been against this much. He was jubilant. Goddamn, this was one great afternoon!

Wendell was pulling the battered Plymouth into the pit lane when someone hit him hard from behind. It was Beau Welles. Figuring that he had lost his brakes, Wendell speeded up, but then Welles rammed him again, forcing the Plymouth into the wall, and he knew it was no accident. Okay! he thought. He crawled out through the Plymouth's window, ready to nail Welles and nail him good. Welles sat there in his car, smirking.

Bubba White got to him first. 'Beau,' said Bubba, 'just what in the goddamn hell is the idea of wrecking me? Man, you just about totalled my car!'

Welles just looked at him.

'You deaf, man?' Bubba shouted. 'Don't sit there with that shit-eating grin! I said, you just about totalled my car!'

'You don't understand,' said Welles. 'I wasn't aiming for you. I was trying to hit the nigger.'

The explanation did not calm Bubba. 'Boy,' he yelled, 'you better learn to drive before you go trying anything like that again. Look at my *car*!'

'It's too damn bad about – ' Welles started to say, and then Bubba hauled him out of his car through the window, using just one arm, and hit him in the mouth.

Wendell stepped aside to enjoy the action. He still wanted a piece of Welles for himself, but he could afford to wait and see what would be left when Bubba got done.

Didn't look as if there was going to be much left, Wendell judged after a minute. Bubba White was now working on Welles like a one-man demolition crew. Bubba was just about taking Welles to pieces. Wendell had never seen anything quite like this calculated destruction. He felt a little bit sick at his stomach.

As he turned away from the spectacle, he saw a man with a monkey wrench running across the infield and recognized him as a friend of Beau Welles's. That monkey wrench was clearly meant for Bubba White's head. Wendell stepped forward and decked the running man.

Fans had come pouring out of the grandstand to get in on the fight, and the pit lane was crowded now. Bubba propped Welles neatly up against the side of his car and stepped aside, wanting no part of what was fast becoming a free-for-all. Wendell had the same idea. His eyes met Bubba's as they retreated toward the infield.

'Thanks,' said Bubba.

'Yeah, you too,' said Wendell. He had a feeling that

this was a man he could get along with. They were in the same business, after all.

'You planning to race again anytime soon?' Bubba asked him. 'Maybe I could give you a few pointers.'

XII

A few days later Wendell was out in his backyard again, working on the Plymouth, trying to repair the damages inflicted on it by the race. He had some pretty good ideas about how to get the accelerator pedal to stay on, and about improving the hand throttle, just in case. There was probably no point in trying to do anything about the damage to the car's body. If those drivers were going to go after him like that in every race, he might as well save his time. Still, he liked to have his cars look pretty. He figured he'd do something about the worst of it when he had time. He was underneath the Plymouth when Peewee came around the house.

'Hey, how you doing?' Peewee asked.

'Hand me that wrench, will you?' Wendell asked. 'I'm doing fine. Getting things set so she won't come apart on me next time.'

'It was too bad about that.' Peewee handed him the wrench. 'You were doing good for a while. Hey, tell me, man, what was it *really* like out there?'

Smiling, Wendell pulled himself out from under the Plymouth. 'I'll tell you, Peewee,' he said, 'it was root hog or die.' Then he noticed the large man standing behind Peewee, a truly big man. Makes old Peewee look about the size of a peanut, Wendell thought. The big man returned his nod.

'Want you to meet a friend of mine,' said Peewee. 'This is Woodrow Wilson Taylor. Used to have a gas station over by Narrow Bridge.'

Wendell wiped the grease off his hand and reached out to shake. 'Good to meet you,' Taylor said slowly. 'Saw you race Sunday and figured that maybe you could use a good mechanic to help you out in the pits.'

Wendell looked doubtful. This man talked slow and had the slowest handshake in the world, and he looked too damn big to get under any car Wendell had ever seen. 'You've got to be fast to work in the pits,' he said.

Taylor opened his mouth, but Peewee spoke first. 'Old Woodrow's so fast he's a blur,' he said.

Taylor closed his mouth. It took him about a minute, it seemed to Wendell. He simply couldn't believe that this man could work fast. Still, there was no getting around the fact that he needed a mechanic.

'Okay,' Wendell said. 'We got a race in Cluster Springs next week. Then there's a race over in Roanoke the week after that. I'm going to try to enter them both. You want to come along?'

'Sounds good to me,' Taylor said. Wendell hoped his slow speech wasn't catching. Telephone lines would be tied up all over town, all day and all night, if everyone took as long to get out three-four words as this man did.

'Cluster Springs? Roanoke?' said Peewee. 'How come we're going so far away when there's another race in Danville right next Sunday?'

'After all that trouble,' Wendell explained, 'old Billy Joe isn't so sure that it's a real good idea having me around. But he told me that he'd fix it up for Cluster Springs – the promoter there is a friend of his – and then maybe I can come back to the Speedway when things have cooled down a little. Seems like that fight Sunday damaged some property as well as some people, and Billy Joe wants to get the Speedway repaired so folks can tear it down again.' He laughed. 'Besides, you know how much I made driving Sunday? Exactly nothing. And Bubba White told me that at Roanoke everybody gets a share of the purse, win or lose, even if he doesn't finish in the top three. If I'm going to make a living doing this, I better start getting paid pretty damn soon.'

'What about Roanoke?' Peewee asked. 'Billy Joe fix that up, too?'

'Nope,' Wendell replied.

Peewee shook his head. 'Then what makes you think you can get on the track there?'

Wendell smiled. 'Bubba White gave me the promoter's name, so I just called him up. Told him I'd been racing here, and he said to come on over to Roanoke.'

Peewee was impressed – here was Wendell talking like he'd been dealing with promoters all his life. He'd never thought of Wendell as much of a businessman before. He himself had handled most of the business part of the bootlegging.

Wendell turned to Woodrow Taylor. 'Okay,' he said, 'let's you and me get started. What do your friends call you? Woody?'

Taylor considered a while. 'Woodrow,' he said.

'I thought they might,' Wendell said.

Peewee went off for a cup of coffee with Mary, leaving Wendell to size up his new mechanic. Woodrow compressed himself under the Plymouth, discussed its problems, and called out for tools. It seemed like he really did know more than a little something about cars, and Wendell began to feel pretty happy as the afternoon wore on. By suppertime, the car looked a whole lot better.

Peewee came and collected Woodrow at about five o'clock. Clearly, Mary hadn't asked him to stay for supper. Not like her, Wendell thought, as he said good-bye, giving Peewee a quick handshake and Woodrow a slow one.

In the kitchen, where Mary was already starting to dish up supper, he said, 'Hey, honey, we running out of food? I thought you might want to invite Peewee and my new mechanic to eat with us.'

'I didn't want any company,' Mary said. 'Wendell, I want to talk to you. Just you, personally, and none of your friends or family butting in and telling me what to think.' Then she was silent for a while.

Wendell watched her as they began to eat. He wondered if he hadn't been taking her too much for granted. She was always there, cooking meals, taking care of the house, of the kids. He loved her, and he didn't want to hurt her, but there wasn't any way that he could do what he had to do without her worrying.

'Honey, I know what you're thinking,' he said. 'But look here, now, I've got me a start. I've been in a race – and I finished it – and I'm going to have a better chance over at Cluster Springs. And at Roanoke, I'll bring home some money, no matter what.'

'It isn't the money,' Mary said. 'And you know how

happy I was that you got the chance to race. But Wendell, there at the Speedway – those white drivers just plain tried to kill you. Seems like even running liquor might be safer, and God knows that scares me enough.'

'Look, woman,' he said. 'That down at the Speedway was nothing. We both know the cops have been trying to shoot me full of holes for a long time now. And we both know that I can take care of myself. I'd rather stand up against a cat with a wrench than a cat with a badge and a gun, any day. And this may be my one chance – hauling liquor isn't getting any easier, and I don't know how to do anything besides drive and fix cars.'

'You could open a garage,' she said.

'With what?' Wendell asked. 'Besides, I'm not going to give up just when I'm getting started. Look, if I'm not any good at it, I'll stop. But I have to find out. You wouldn't want me to quit now, and have all those white boys laughing over how I haven't got the guts to face up to them?'

Mary knew he had guts. She just didn't want to see them spread out all over some raceway. Those crowds were there for blood, and she didn't want Wendell to give up one drop. She thought about Sunday and tried to decide which had been worse, the driving or the fight. She'd been glad to see Wendell walking off, talking to that white driver, looking as if he didn't have a care in the world. But it was that carelessness that really worried her.

'I'll always provide for you and the kids,' Wendell was going on, 'one way or another. But right now I've got to race. And I can win. I know I can.'

She cleared off the plates, and he noticed that she hadn't eaten much. He pushed his chair away and went over to where she stood at the sink, rinsing the dishes. He gave her a big hug, hoping she'd find comfort in it.

'They'll kill you,' Mary said slowly, 'before they'll let you win.'

XIII

The stands at Cluster Springs were packed the following Sunday. The promoter there, Scooter Davis, had taken Billy Joe's advice and promoted the hell out of having a black driver. This Sunday Wendell arrived more in style – Peewee had got hold of a huge black Packard, and Number Thirty-Four was towed onto the track to great applause from the colored section. And though Wendell was still relying on his old football helmet, he had something like a uniform. He was wearing smartly pressed matching khakis, and Grandma Scott had made him a patch with a big '34' on it. Mary had sewed it on over his left breast pocket.

Compared to Danville, things at Cluster Springs looked pretty professional. Instead of everybody just lining up at the starting line, there were to be three preliminary heats of eight or nine cars each, with the top three from each going into the feature race. Wendell was in the third heat, so he and Woodrow had plenty of time to tinker with the Plymouth.

Peewee stood on the infield and watched as they worked. The other drivers, as if by agreement, pretended that they were invisible – which was just what Wendell had expected, and how he liked it. He glanced up from time to time at the early heats and saw Bubba White go out in the first. Damn shame it wasn't Beau Welles, he thought. He didn't like the thought of having to play games with that mean bastard again. It was a surprise that Welles came to be racing today, considering the terrific working-over White had given him just a week ago. Cat's just as tough as he looks, Wendell decided, then went back to making fine adjustments on the Plymouth carburetor.

His luck was good in his qualifying heat. Five cars tangled on the opening lap, and from there on, he and the two other remaining drivers just tooled around nice and easy, sure of their places in the big race. Neither of the other survivors even tried to bang him up – they were saving their cars for later.

Wendell drew up onto the infield, so that he and Woodrow could make a last-minute check of the car, and a few minutes later he looked up from his tinkering and saw Bubba White standing beside him. He was surprised. If it took nerve for him, Wendell Scott, to be on that infield, it took twice as much nerve for White to be seen having anything to do with him. But then he remembered what White had done to Beau Welles, and figured that White simply didn't have to give a shit about what anyone thought.

'Hey, Scott,' White said. He looked inside the Plymouth, and nodded approvingly. 'Looks real good.'

'Hey, White,' Wendell said. 'How you doing? What happened out there on the backstretch? Looked like you really wrecked, man.'

'Damn axle broke,' White said. 'There I was, pretty as a picture, in second place, when *bam!* Damn thing let loose, and there I was heading straight into the damn wall.'

Woodrow moved around to check the Plymouth's rear axle. No point in not learning from someone else's misfortune.

'Anyway,' White went on, 'my car is totalled. So seeing as I have some spare time on my hands, I thought I'd come over and see if any of you-all wanted a hand.'

Goddamn, thought Wendell, but this old Bubba White's something else. 'Thanks,' he said. 'It'll be real nice having you. I need all the help I can get.'

Woodrow nodded in agreement. Since Peewee didn't do anything except watch other people work, he could use an extra hand – even a white one.

'One more thing,' said White. 'About this promoter, this Scooter Davis. Well, he doesn't promote around here so much any more, but there are two or three of us who remember when he did. He's been known to run out with the loot when he thinks he can get away with it.'

'Well, son of a bitch,' Wendell said. 'What happens then?'

'What happens is that we're ready for him. My cousin Larry's up there in the stands, and he's going to be watching Davis, not the race. If he sees Davis fixing to light out before the payoff, Larry's going to wave a big rebel flag. Then I'll signal you all from the pits, and you go after Davis's ass.'

'You really expect him to try something?' Wendell asked.

'It wouldn't surprise me at all,' White said. 'Look at those stands, man. He's making an extra gate having you run, and it might be that he won't be able to resist the temptation. Good luck,' he added, as the starter signalled Wendell to the line.

Wendell drew a position in the middle of the pack, made the parade lap, then really hit it when the green flag dropped. The car was running smooth as a whistle, the engine sounded strong, and, though he was still getting slammed around some by the other drivers, he was dishing out as good as he got. He kept an especially sharp eye on Beau Welles, but Welles seemed to be behaving himself – at least he wasn't trying any more kamikaze raids. With four laps left, Wendell was up in third place. Going to take me home some money today, he thought.

Suddenly Bubba White jumped out of the pit, waving the checkered flag that he'd seized from a startled track official. By the time the official got the flag back, all but one of the cars had roared right off the track. And with three laps still to go. The official wondered what in all hell was happening, and so did the crowd.

Wendell made one more lap, then slowed down so that Bubba White could climb aboard. Then he floorboarded it, hightailing it off the track after the others. One way or another, he damned well was going to take some money home today!

When Wendell caught up with the pack, there was so much dust that he couldn't see quite what they were chasing, but he knew who – Scooter Davis. There wasn't much other traffic on the country road that led from the track, and it was a damn good thing, he thought, as a jalopy full of teenagers swerved out of the way and into a ditch. Then he saw the big Chrysler convertible, and Scooter Davis in it.

Davis had been feeling fine. He'd had a good take – five thousand dollars – and every penny of it was in the cashbox on the seat beside him. He was heading for Maryland to check out a track there. As long as he kept moving around, he figured, he could make a pretty good thing out of this promoting business. Just then he saw the cloud of dust rising behind him. It looked like a tornado, but it wasn't the right shape. Davis checked his speedometer. He was within the legal limit, so if it was the cops on his tail, they couldn't bother him. He looked at the dust cloud again and realized it wasn't the cops. Jesus Christ, he thought. It's the racers! He gunned his engine, hoping against hope that he could outrun the stock cars, or that they'd spin out and send each other off the road, or that an angel with a flaming sword would appear to save him.

It didn't take long for the race cars to overtake the Chrysler and force it into the ditch. Davis cut the engine and sat still, praying, as the cars screamed to a stop, twisting across the road at every possible angle. He was too scared even to pray when the drivers converged upon him, a number of them carrying wrenches.

Wendell hung back, watching, as the other drivers began to demolish the Chrysler.

The drivers worked methodically, for all their screaming and swearing. They started with the wheels, then removed the hood, the trunk lid, the fenders, the carburetor, the doors, the rear seat, and the steering wheel. They reduced the car to a skeleton, leaving Davis to sit quaking in the front seat, which was about all that was left.

'Hey, boys, don't be mad,' Davis pleaded. He held the cashbox out to Bubba White. 'You want the money? Here, take it. I wasn't trying to cheat you-all. I was going to send off the prizes in the mail.' He knew that nobody was going to believe him. 'But please don't hurt me,' he went on. 'I'm a veteran of World War Two! Got shot up in the Pacific! Got me a wife and kids at home!'

Beau Welles handed Davis the Chrysler's oil filter. Then he put the air cooler over his head, with considerable force. Bubba White counted out the money, dividing it among the drivers. When he was finished, Bubba carefully replaced the cashbox beside the dazed Davis on the front seat.

Wendell and Bubba laughed all the way back to Cluster Springs. Wendell couldn't wait to tell Peewee what he'd missed. Goddamn, but old Davis had looked comical, sitting there in what was left of his car! And it was nice to have the money, too!

XIV

A week later Wendell, Peewee, and Woodrow set out for Roanoke. They were again in the big black Packard, towing the Plymouth, now so modified that it looked like all the other 'stock' cars.

'Hey, Wendell,' the little man said, 'what if this Roanoke promoter tries to pull a runout on you, like Scooter Davis? What'll you guys do to *him*?'

'Bubba White says this promoter – name's Thurlough – is on the level,' Wendell said. 'Roanoke's a big town, compared to Cluster Springs, and he's been running the races there for years.'

'Well, we'll soon see,' said Peewee.

Wendell kept looking back over his shoulder to make sure that the racer was still attached to the car. Roanoke was getting pretty close to the big time, he thought. There'd be money if he won here or no, and if he should just happen to win, there'd be more than money. If he won at Roanoke – why, people would start hearing about him at dirt tracks all over the South!

Woodrow was asleep in the back seat when the big Packard turned into the drivers' entrance of the Roanoke Speedway and stopped on the infield. 'I'm going to find the promoter,' said Wendell, getting out of the car. 'You wake up Woodrow and unhook the racer.'

A bunch of white drivers were standing around talking, and Wendell went up to them. 'Excuse me,' he said, 'can you tell me where I can find Mr Thurlough?'

The men just stared at him. Wendell repeated his question, and after considering for a while, one driver pointed to a group over by the pits. 'That's Thurlough,' he said. 'Little guy with the glasses, right over there.' The drivers watched Wendell walk away, not quite believing their eyes – here was a colored man, with what looked like a uniform and a helmet, and be damned if that didn't look like a racing car over there!

Wendell walked up to the man with the spectacles. 'Mr Thurlough?' he said. 'Excuse me, my name's Scott. Wendell Scott. That's my car over there – that Plymouth, Number Thirty-Four.'

Thurlough stared at him.

'You remember I called you from Danville,' Wendell went on, 'and you told me to come on over.' Thurlough still didn't say anything. Goddamn, Wendell began to wonder, is this man stone deaf?

Thurlough took his arm and led him away from the pits, looking back over his shoulder three or four times. When he was sure they were out of earshot of the other drivers, he said, 'Mr Scott, I'm truly sorry, but I can't let you run on this track. Not today, anyway. Other boys would all walk off it.'

'But you told me to come on over,' Wendell said, getting angry. He wondered if this had been Bubba White's notion of a joke, but Bubba wasn't that mean, for all his roughness.

'You tricked me, boy,' said Thurlough, sounding aggrieved. 'I couldn't *see* you over the telephone.' He saw the look on Wendell's face and began looking around, in case he needed help. 'Now, don't get me wrong,' he went on. 'I've got nothing against you colored people. Nothing at all. In fact, I was thinking of letting a bunch of you stage a race here one day among yourselves.'

Wendell felt like smashing the little man right in the mouth. Too angry to say a word, he turned on his heel and walked back toward his car. Peewee and Woodrow both saw trouble coming, and when he saw Thurlough following Wendell, Peewee reached for a wrench. He reckoned he and Thurlough were about the same size, so it would be a fair fight. And whatever was happening, Wendell had better leave the action up to him. Wendell looked like he just might kill somebody.

Thurlough caught up to Wendell as he reached the Plymouth. 'Listen,' he said, 'I've got an idea. There are a lot of boys here today who can drive, but don't have cars. Why don't you let me get one of them to drive your car for you? That way your trip here won't have been for nothing.'

Peewee tightened his grip on the wrench, but Wendell's voice was calm – almost too calm. 'Look here, Mr Thurlough,' he said. 'I built this car. Myself. With my own two hands. And I drive it!'

Thurlough backed off. 'What's the matter with him? That boy's crazy!' he said to no one in particular.

The rage exploded inside Wendell. By God, he *was* going to drive his car and he was going to drive it here! He snapped on his helmet and crawled through the window. Woodrow and Peewee jumped out of the way as he fired up the engine and headed across the infield to the track.

A few drivers were out warming their cars, showing off for the fans, doing easy laps. Wendell roared past them, and one or two thought that the race had already begun somehow, without their noticing it. They took off after Wendell, but soon fell back. Number Thirty-Four, whoever the hell he was, was really making time!

After five laps at a boiling pace, Wendell blew his engine and coasted to a stop near the grandstands. His rage was pretty much spent, and he was suddenly tired. He crawled out of the Plymouth and took off his helmet. His face was so streaked with the dirt of the track that none of the fans could have made out what color he'd been originally. Not that any of them expected a black driver today, Wendell thought. Old Thurlough sure didn't advertise it. He looked at the colored section of the stands and noted with satisfaction that it was almost empty. Maybe Thurlough'd learn sometime soon that having a black driver could make him some money. But for now, Wendell thought, I've shown him I can drive.

Peewee pulled the Packard up beside him, and Woodrow got out and began to hook up the racing car. Two white spectators came over to get a closer look at Number Thirty-Four and its wild-assed driver, then retreated in confusion.

'Did you see that?' one of them asked his friend. 'That guy's got him a colored pit crew. Never seen anything like it.'

'It's not just a colored pit crew,' the other man said. 'That's a colored driver.'

'Shit, no, it can't be,' said the first man. 'There aren't any colored drivers.'

The Packard, with the Plymouth in tow, started off the track. Woodrow was asleep in the back seat before it had even reached the 'Exit' sign. Peewee and Wendell did not look back.

XV

For a long time, heading back to Danville, they sat in silence. Once in a while Wendell looked back to check the racer. Peewee drove, and Woodrow slept like a baby. Suddenly they were brought to attention by the persistent honking of a car that was following them at more than a safe distance.

'Pull over, Peewee,' Wendell said, and when the Packard had eased onto the shoulder he got out to take a look at what might be the matter. The chain towing the car was breaking down; its links were being pulled apart. Must have been swerving like a bastard, he thought. No wonder those people were honking. This thing could've killed them if it had broken loose!

'What's the matter?' asked Peewee, joining him.

Wendell shouted at him. 'On top of everything else! Of all the goddamn shit! The bar's broke and the goddamn chain is busting! Can't you guys do anything right?'

Peewee knew that this wrath was not really directed at him. 'Calm down, my man,' he said. 'You still fuming from that smart-ass promoter. Now, you just remember that you've already been in two races, and for a black boy from Danville, that's doing pretty good. And we all know you're going to race some more. But you are also going to have to put up with a whole lot more shit before you get recognized. Do you take my meaning?'

Wendell nodded, feeling ashamed about his bad temper.

They got a rope from the Packard and lashed the Plymouth racer on as best they could. Wendell tugged on it, testing. 'All right,' he said. 'Looks like it's going to be okay. But somebody's going to have to sit in it and steer. Peewee, you just volunteered.

Peewee didn't care for the idea. Rope breaks, he

thought, and there I'll be in a car with no engine, and my ass right out where anything coming down the road can knock it off. 'Hey, man,' he said. 'Why me? What about Sleeping Beauty in there?'

Wendell laughed. 'Old Woodrow's so sound asleep it'd take dynamite to wake him up. Besides, he's too big to fit in through the window. You just get right in, Peewee – you're about to become the *second* black racing driver in the history of Danville!' He gave his friend a good slap on the rump, as the little man wiggled into the racer.

Wendell drove the Packard slowly back onto the road. The racer followed without any trouble. It looked like the rope would hold, but he proceeded cautiously. Of all things in the world, he didn't want to lose both his racing car *and* his best friend.

They were driving through a small town when Woodrow came to life in the back seat. 'Let's get us something to eat and drink,' he said.

Wendell pointed to the rear window with his thumb, and Woodrow turned and saw Peewee in the racing car. Peewee waved. He was beginning to look happy.

'What's he doing out there?' Woodrow asked.

Wendell explained, and Woodrow said, 'Next thing we do is get us a real tow bar. That is, after we get something to eat.' He looked out the window for a restaurant or diner, but they were in what was clearly a white town. 'Nothing around here. But Wendell, look over there – what do you see?'

'Railroad tracks,' said Wendell.

'That's right,' said Woodrow. 'Now any time you want to find colored folks what do you do?'

'You just follow the railroad tracks,' Wendell laughed, and turned off toward the tracks. Within a few minutes, they found themselves in what was either a small black town or the black section of some bigger place. They passed a square, with a statue of a World War One infantryman in it. A bunch of kids were playing around the base of the statue, but when they saw the Packard and the Plymouth, they stopped to stare. A few of the bolder ones followed, as Wendell slowly circled the square and found a place big enough to park the two cars. Some adults joined the staring children, and by the time Wendell and

Woodrow got out of the Packard, there was a small crowd. Curtains moved in house and store windows and people came out onto their porches for a better look.

A real hero's welcome, thought Wendell. But it was Peewee who was playing the part of the hero, and he was making the most of it.

Peewee popped his head out of the racer, enjoying the 'oooh's' and 'aaah's' that greeted him, knowing that he was the first black race driver these people had ever seen. He hoisted himself out of the window and fell flat on his face. The crowd divided – some giggled and some cheered. Wendell went to pick up his friend, but Peewee spurned him and went on playing his part. He waved to the crowd, then gave the Plymouth an encouraging pat. More people came into the square, and he waved again, in case anybody had missed the first time.

Wendell was leaning up against the racer when a man in a white coat approached him. The man was dressed like a barber, but he was dignified enough to be at least the mayor, Wendell thought.

'This yours?' the man asked, touching the Plymouth with great respect.

'Sure it's mine,' said Wendell. 'Name's Wendell Scott. And that over there is my pit man, Woodrow Wilson Taylor. That other cat's my friend Peewee.'

The barber looked impressed. 'You race that thing against white men?'

At Wendell's nod, a murmur went up from the crowd. Now they were *all* impressed.

'Hear that?' the barber said to the crowd. 'This man's a racing driver.' He held out his hand to Wendell. 'Mr Scott, I'm pleased to meet you. My name is George Allington.'

Wendell smiled and shook Allington's hand. He was suddenly surrounded by hands, and he shook them all, as orderly as he could. The barber stood beside him, directing traffic. 'Wendell Scott,' he said. 'Damn, but that's a familiar name. You any kin to the Scott that hauls liquor around Danville?'

Peewee broke in. 'That's him. *He's* the one and only Wendell Scott. Ask any policeman around Danville or out in the county!'

'You run liquor *and* race cars?' Allington asked Wendell solemnly. 'You ain't looking forward to old age, are you, son?'

'Yes, sir,' said Wendell. 'I've got a family to feed, and the racing itself doesn't come cheap.'

'Well,' Allington said, 'if you can race this thing like you drive those liquor cars, you should make a fortune.'

'That's exactly what we plan to do,' Peewee chimed in, glad to have a chance to get back on the center of the stage. 'Isn't it, Woodrow?'

Woodrow was trying to shoo away some of the small boys who had begun to climb all over the racing car, but there were too many of them. Anyhow, why spoil their fun? Woodrow was still hungry and thirsty, but it didn't look like they'd have much chance of getting to a café as long as they were the center of attention. He allowed Peewee to pose him with Wendell in front of the car as box cameras were brought out.

A patrol car circled the square, but only the people on the outer edges of the crowd bothered to look at it.

'Looks like a racing car,' the driver said to his partner. 'But what the hell's it doing in Niggertown?'

'Maybe the niggers stole one!' the partner laughed. 'Tell you what, let's go see. Maybe we can have us a little fun, whatever it is.'

The car's radio came to life. 'Car Three,' the dispatcher's voice said. 'Car Three. There is a cow reported in the street at Main and Fifth. Repeat. There is a cow in the street . . . '

The driver picked up the microphone, cutting off the radio voice. 'Roger, Central. We're on our way, Main and Fifth.' He turned to his partner. 'It's probably the damn heifer of McCoy's again.'

As the patrol car swung away from the square, the driver got another good look at what had drawn the crowd. Wendell, with his helmet on now, was posing in front of the racer for the kids to take his picture.

'That *was* a race car,' the driver said. 'I swear to God it was. And the driver was a nigger.'

'Couldn't be,' said his partner. 'There ain't any nigger drivers.'

BOOK III

I

Roanoke was the last time anyone turned Wendell away. By the time Mary had their fifth baby, a third girl, he had begun to drive all over the South. And he was winning, too. But the game was changing. What had once been a sport for outlaw drivers on outlaw tracks was becoming a million-dollar business. With the opening, in 1950, of the Darlington raceway, the big companies in automobiles, oil, and accessories became sponsors, and speed became a matter of money as well as guts. And the Grand National Series, inaugurated by the National Association for Stock Car Auto Racing, turned the sport into a year-round activity, not just something for an occasional Sunday afternoon. The new breed of driver was thoroughly professional, concerned with business; of the old, wild breed, only a few were still racing – among them Wendell, Bubba White, and Beau Welles. The cool new men didn't seem to have much use for them. It was a safer, better regulated sport, but some fans and drivers thought it was a hell of a lot less fun.

Wendell was doing well; he had even beaten the famous Richard Petty a few times. But he still hadn't made it all the way to the top. He knew he had the talent – he'd always known that – but he couldn't get the money or any meaningful sponsorship. Wendell knew that many races Petty ran cost his sponsor more than the purse, but that the publicity was worth it. He knew that Petty had never driven an unsponsored car, although Petty's father had been one of the good-old-boys and had driven plenty of them. But no factory was going to put up the funds to back a black driver on Southern tracks in what remained essentially a Southern sport, and Wendell knew that, too.

So he worked on his own cars, without a big company

behind him, depended on his friends for his pit crew, and ran a little liquor now and then. By the time his kids were old enough to crew for him, they were also going to be old enough for college, and he and Mary were determined that they should go – *all* of them, including Sybil, who was still in diapers.

But the bootlegging business still paid good money, and Wendell hadn't had any real trouble since that Christmas years ago, though Sheriff Cotten came by every now and again, and the house was still watched a lot of the time. It made Mary fretful. And she certainly didn't want the boys following in their daddy's footsteps.

One day, working out back of the house on a racing car – he preferred Fords these days – Wendell found himself chuckling at the recollection of a scene that had taken place when Sheriff Cotten had dropped by 'for a chat'. Debbie, who wasn't too far out of diapers, had beat Mary to the door, taken one look, and slammed it right in the sheriff's face. Mary had chided her, but Wendell thought she was a fast learner. 'Now, don't you dare say a thing to encourage her,' Mary told him sternly. And he hadn't. And there was the day he had come home to find that Wendell, Jr., and Frankie had discovered the cigar box in which he hid his collection of ignition keys. The keys were spread out all over the living-room carpet and Wendell had had to collect them again and find a new hiding place. Wendell mopped his brow. It was a damn good thing that Cotten hadn't chosen to drop by on that particular day.

He studied the Ford he was working on. He'd had plenty of chances to examine the factory-backed models, and he'd become aware of techniques that he'd never be able to duplicate in the backyard. Acid-dipping, for instance, so that the body metal was etched down to the thinnest possible shell. How the hell could he do that at home? Of course, one of those light cars wouldn't have lasted ten minutes in any of the early races he'd been in, but now there wasn't as much deliberate bammin' and frammin' – not even when he was driving. Sure, he could, and did, incorporate on his own racers the safety features of the newer cars, but he simply couldn't match the sophistication of the factory teams' equipment. Still, he was racing regularly, even if he hadn't yet made the Grand National Series. On a short track anywhere he was still a force to be reckoned with.

Wendell backed up for a good look at the Ford, wondering if there was anything more to do before he painted the number thirty-four on the sides. From the kitchen, Mary called to ask if he wanted a cup of coffee, and he gave her a good look, too, when she brought it out to him. Five kids, he thought, and still got a figure like a schoolgirl. Still the prettiest girl in Danville. It didn't seem possible that they'd been married for more than ten years.

'Honey,' he said, 'do you want to come to the race over in Spartanburg next week?'

Mary shook her head. She hardly ever went to the races. There were the kids to take care of – and there was her fear of the danger to Wendell. 'I just can't do it, baby,' she said. 'Not with Sybil teething and all.'

'Maybe next time,' Wendell said. He set the coffee down on the hood of the Ford so that he could give her a good, two-handed hug. She was a strong-minded woman, and he knew how she felt.

II

The Spartanburg race turned out to be one of the most memorable that Wendell ever drove. And it provided Peewee with one of his finest hours.

It was a beautiful April afternoon, and the black section of the stands was full to capacity. And every man, woman, and child in that section screamed when Wendell got out in front. He still had fifty laps to go, but his lead was a commanding one. When he saw Peewee signal forty-five laps, he was still ahead, and feeling good. But the track was getting slick, and he knew he'd have to watch out, especially on the short chute leading toward the pits. There was a concrete wall there, just waiting to jump out and wreck him if he got careless.

Beau Welles was behind him, and he began to close up as they rushed into the first turn. Wendell drove the accelerator pedal to the floorboards, and Welles let up at the last instant. But Wendell had gotten himself sucked in too deep – the tires couldn't get any more bite and the car began to drift up into the wall. It seemed to take forever. He tapped it pretty good, and when he eased the Ford down off the wall it was smoking heavily. Shit, he thought, the damn radiator must have split! And with forty-five laps to go, he'd thrown away a clear win. He'd been four laps ahead. *Four laps.* He was disgusted with himself as he limped to the pits.

Woodrow and Peewee were standing by. Woodrow had the hood open before the Ford even stopped and immediately confirmed Wendell's diagnosis. 'We're in trouble! Radiator's had it.'

As Wendell hauled himself out of the window of the Ford, Peewee grabbed him by the arm. 'Come on, let's go,' he shouted. 'I got me an idea.' He hustled Wendell out of the pits and across the infield. Before the black section of the stands, Peewee brought them both to a sharp stop. He made a megaphone of his hands. 'Okay, everybody,' he yelled. 'I need me a Ford radiator for about twenty minutes!'

I'll be damned, thought Wendell. If they only had time it just might work. These folks had been cheering him on all afternoon – some of them had been cheering him on for years – and they were sure as hell on his side. Peewee was really exhorting the crowd, now, working them up.

'Who's the lucky man?' shouted Peewee, making sure to drown out the roar of the cars that were still circling the track. 'Who's the lucky man who's going to temporarily donate his Ford radiator to our man Wendell Scott?' He waved his arms. 'Ain't got all day! He can't do it without you! One lousy little radiator!'

Three men stood up in the stands and began to move toward the front.

'Bring it back as good as new,' Peewee yelled. 'Better than new! You can tell all your friends that *Wendell Scott* used your radiator – to win!' He jumped up and down like a cheerleader. 'Let's hear it for a Ford radiator! Let's hear it for our man Wendell Scott!'

Wendell recognized one of the men who had come forward. It was the barber, George Allington, who had been one of his most faithful fans ever since Wendell and his crew, on the way back from Roanoke, had brought a little excitement to the dusty town square. Wendell didn't forget a face, especially not a face that showed up Sunday after Sunday, the year round, at any track between Roanoke and Danville. 'Hey, Allington!' he shouted. 'See you out in the parking lot!'

He grabbed Peewee and ran with him across the infield to the exit tunnel. This brought them out near the entrance to the colored section of the stands, and they got there just as George Allington arrived with two other men. They all ran together to where Allington's car was parked. It took them only about a minute to get the radiator out of Allington's Ford sedan. By the time Allington had slammed down the hood, the others, carrying the radiator, were following Wendell and Peewee back toward the tunnel. Allington caught up with them in the pit, where Woodrow was installing the borrowed radiator in the racer. Allington watched Wendell crawl in through the racer's window and grinned when the car started with a great roar. His radiator was going to be famous!

Wendell tore onto the tracks like a maniac, surprised by Peewee's parting shout of 'Thirty laps!' It had taken less than ten minutes, by his figuring, to borrow and install the new radiator. I'll be damned, he thought. Good old Allington! Ten minutes was a lot of time to lose, but from the way the other cars were skidding around on the oily track, Wendell thought he might have a chance of ending up in the money. He lapped Bubba White and began moving up into the pack. He was going to have to lap Bubba and all the rest a hell of a lot more times before he regained the lead, and that was going to take some hard chasing. He soon moved up behind Bubba again, drafting him, and the others, for all it was worth. Peewee gave him a 'thumbs up' sign from the pit.

Wendell drove like a man possessed for the last few laps. His luck held, and he made use of every trick he knew, lapping the leaders time and again. He was in second place when the checkered flag came down, but from the jubilation in the colored grandstand, and the jubilation in the pit when he pulled up, it was damn near as good as winning.

Woodrow reached through the window and grabbed his hand. Allington was reaching for him, too, half crazy with the near-victory. Wendell crawled out of the window and was surrounded by smiling and shouting friends. 'We're on our way,' Peewee whooped.

Damned if it didn't look as if it might be true, Wendell thought. Word of this race gets around, maybe I'll get me some sponsorship money.

Peewee disappeared into the crowd of fans who were now mobbing the infield and the pit. In a minute he was back, an arm around each of two good-looking girls. Wendell couldn't hear their names over the noise and the congratulations, but he got a nice smile from them and saw Peewee's big grin. The little man must have some kind of magic about him, Wendell thought, the way he seemed to score one hundred percent of the time. As

Peewee led the girls over to Woodrow, he saw Bubba White coming toward him through the crowd. Earlier that day he'd let Bubba have a spare rear end for his car and lent him Woodrow to install it, but there had been no time for visiting then or since.

Bubba stuck out his hand. 'Hey, Scott,' he said. 'That was one hell of a race you ran. Man! I just about couldn't believe it, those last few laps. Seemed like every time I looked up, there you were again, right on my tail and then right up front. You kept me out of the money, boy! But hell, if it hadn't been for you I wouldn't have been out there at all today. I surely do appreciate the use of that rear end.'

'Thanks, Bubba, and you're welcome,' Wendell said, shouting to make himself heard over the noisy crowd.

'How about supper – on me? I got me a certificate for two free steak dinners for making the fastest qualifying time.'

'That sounds right good,' Wendell said. He called over to his crew. 'Hey, Peewee, you mind if me and – '

'You just do whatever you want,' Peewee yelled back. He pointed to the girls. 'Me and Woodrow's got plans! *Big plans!*'

Wendell winked at him, then turned back to Bubba. 'Okay, Bubba,' he said. 'Give me about half an hour to get washed up and to return Mr Allington his radiator.'

Bubba looked surprised. 'Return Mr Allington's radiator?'

'Tell you all about it at supper,' Wendell promised. He opened up the hood of the car and began to disconnect the radiator. George Allington came over to watch, delighted as could be. 'There she is,' Wendell said, 'good as new.'

'Better than new,' said Allington, and he laughed fit to die.

III

Wendell and Bubba understood each other as drivers and as men, and they respected each other. They both knew that they were survivors of an earlier era, when racing stock cars was the province of farmboys and wild-assed bootleggers, and this drew them closer together. Like Wendell, Bubba still made his own equipment, often holding it together with spit. And like Wendell, he still had no sponsor. If the color of Wendell's skin scared off potential backers, Bubba's good-old-boy cussedness scared them, too. Both men had kids to educate, and both were strapped for money to continue racing. So Wendell still hauled a little liquor, and Bubba spent his spare time driving in thrill shows. They could both use a free steak supper.

In the restaurant's parking lot, they looked the place over. Nothing fancy – it looked like a nice, clean, family sort of place. And they were both looking like nice, clean family men – they had cleaned up carefully after the race.

They were still laughing when they entered the cafe; Wendell had been explaining about the radiator swap, and Bubba was making jokes about how he'd get a lawyer and sue. The other customers stared at them as they found a table and sat, but Wendell and Bubba ignored them. They traded old racing jokes for a while, paying no attention to the fact that some customers were leaving. They didn't even see the waitress approach with two glasses of water, take one look, and go right back into the kitchen.

The restaurant's owner, a pleasant-looking lady with blue hair, finally interrupted their storytelling. She was smiling nervously. 'Good evening, gentlemen.'

'Good evening, ma'am,' they replied in unison.

The blue-haired lady cleared her throat and said, as

firmly as she could, 'I'm sorry, but you'll have to leave. We don't serve colored here.' She gestured toward the sign by the cash register. 'We Reserve the Right to Refuse Service to Anyone.'

Wendell started to get up without argument, but Bubba waved him back down. He wondered what Bubba had in mind. If it had been a man who said that, Bubba would most likely hit him. But how would Bubba handle a nice-looking old lady?

Bubba winked at her, and seemed to enjoy her embarrassment. He produced the prize certificate and handed it over.

'Oh dear,' the lady said, blushing as she read it. If she hadn't been holding the certificate, she might have wrung her hands. 'Oh, my! I just don't know *what* to do! We never *have* served colored here. But it does say free steaks . . . Oh, I wish my husband were here,' she dithered on. '*He'd* know what to do.'

Bubba just kept smiling. A prize was a prize, and he'd won it fair, and he was going to get it. Wendell looked straight ahead. He didn't like being in the middle of a scene – maybe he shouldn't have taken Bubba's invitation in the first place – but he was beginning to find the blue-haired lady's distress kind of funny.

She seemed finally to make up her mind. 'I suppose it's all right,' she said. 'This *is* something special, isn't it?'

'Oh mercy, yes,' said Bubba.

The lady leaned close over the table, almost whispering. 'Well, then, I'll fix you boys a steak. But you've got to promise not to do this again.'

Wendell held up his hand as if he were taking the Boy Scout oath, and Bubba crossed his heart. Reassured, the lady went off into the kitchen. But she was back in a minute. 'Excuse me,' she said to Wendell, 'but how do you people eat your meat?'

Wendell gave her his most charming smile. 'Rare,' he said. 'Same way my friend here likes it.'

The waitress gave them each a glass of water. They were about to order beer when they saw Cecil Cooney standing at the bar. Bubba and Wendell knew Cecil Cooney; they had both raced against him one time or another. But Cecil hadn't been driving for quite a while now, and from the look of his belly he'd been spending the time drinking instead. He'd certainly been pouring it down this evening.

Cecil started over toward them, and Bubba got up quickly. Cecil was a known son of a bitch, and it looked like he was spoiling for trouble.

Cecil brushed right by Bubba without a word. He glowered down at Wendell, still not speaking. Well, hell, looks can't kill, Wendell thought. 'Hello, Cooney,' he said.

'Wendell,' Cecil said slowly, 'I always figured that you were a good old boy, but right now I don't like what I'm seeing.'

'Just what don't you like?' Wendell asked.

Cecil pointed vaguely to the remaining white customers. 'Damn it all! You know what I mean.'

Wendell sighed. 'Cooney, the way I look at it, none of this is any of your business.'

'If that's what you think,' Cecil said, 'then you and me better fix it up right now.'

Oh, shit, Wendell thought, all I want is a simple steak dinner. He got up, wondering where to hit Cecil first. The belly looked pretty soft, but he might have a better chance at the head. Bubba picked up an unopened can of beer from a nearby table and tried to calm things down. 'Take it easy, Cecil,' he said. 'Come on, have a beer.' He held the can out to Cecil, who pushed it away.

'You keep out of this, nigger-lover,' Cecil said.

Bubba took careful aim and hit Cecil on the temple with the beer can, and Cecil crumpled like a sack of potatoes. As he fell, a couple of other customers rose in anger.

'Come on, Wendell,' said Bubba, heading for the door. 'I must be getting old. I just don't feel like fighting any more than I have to.'

On their way out they passed the blue-haired lady, who was just coming out of the kitchen with two steaks on a tray.

The next time Bubba and Wendell had supper together, it was at Bubba's house. The time after that, it was at Wendell's. Mary and Bubba's wife, Bobbi, found they had a lot of things to talk about, and the kids got along together just fine.

IV

Wendell was really looking forward to his next race, which was scheduled for Atlanta in about twenty-four hours. It would be his first run in the Grand National Series, his first chance to take on some of the big, factory-backed drivers on their own territory. By now he'd won some fifty or so short track races, and he felt pretty good about his prospects.

It was late afternoon, and he was working with Woodrow on the car he would race in Atlanta, a blue Chevrolet. A front fender needed welding, and Wendell was giving it his personal attention. Damn, he thought, it was hot that afternoon! The sparks flew as he brought the torch against the welding rod, but it seemed as if he couldn't even feel the heat from the torch – the day itself was already so hot. It struck him that the metal of the fender was getting a little too bright; he'd have to let it cool off some, maybe even speed the process up a little. 'Woodrow,' he said, 'get me that can of water from the garage? It's right inside by the door.'

Woodrow moved off into the shade of the garage. It was cool in there, and dark, after the heat and brightness of outside. He lingered for a second, then picked up a bucket and went back out into the dazzling light. He looked admiringly at the Chevrolet.

'It's looking good, Wendell,' he said. 'What is it if you win tomorrow night? Number fifty-one or number fifty-two?'

'Never mind how many wins. It's the eight hundred dollars prize money that's important.' Wendell stepped back from the car. 'Throw that water on there,' he told Woodrow, 'while I get the shocks out – '

Both men reeled back from the force of the blaze as

Woodrow threw the contents of the pail on the hot metal. It was gasoline, not water. The car seemed to explode before their eyes, and Wendell sprinted for the garage to get the extinguisher. He thanked God that they'd been working outside, rather than in the garage itself – the whole building would have gone up like lightning. He ran back with the extinguisher, but it was no use. The Chevrolet was a cinder.

Woodrow looked as if he'd just killed his best friend. He didn't say anything. Wendell sat down on a piece of another car and tried to catalogue the damage. The flash and the smell of burning rubber had brought Mary out of the kitchen, but seeing that Wendell and Woodrow were all right, she stopped on the porch and stared in dismay at what was left of the race car.

Woodrow finally spoke. 'Boss, I thought it was water! I do swear to God that I thought it was water!'

'Sure,' Wendell said. 'Sure.' Woodrow was his friend, his mechanic, his righthand man. He didn't do it on purpose, Wendell thought. *But that goddamn dumb old son of a bitch can't tell gasoline from water!* 'Don't feel bad, Woodrow,' he said.

Wendell went on staring at the charred hulk of what had once been a shiny blue Chevrolet. The body seemed completely destroyed, and the tires were burned away. The remains of the car sat on the rims, clouds of acrid smoke still swirling lazily in the air. The engine and drive train were still intact, but what good were they without a body to install them in? Wendell looked at the car parts distributed about him in the yard and wondered if there were enough to start from scratch. Even if there was enough time. He felt tired as hell.

Peewee came over, speechless for a change. Wendell didn't even greet him; Woodrow gave him only a nod.

Wendell finally spoke. 'Come on, Woodrow,' he said. 'Let's get a chain on this thing and tow it out of the way.'

Eager to do anything to help out, Woodrow went over to the charred car and started to lift up the front. It seemed almost to fly out of his hand. Its lightness was amazing. Wendell came over, and between them they were able to move the car bare-handed. It seemed as light as a feather.

'Well, I'll be goddamned,' said Wendell, realizing what had happened. The metal of the car had been oxidized, etched out by the burning. All the sheet was now as thin as on any factory racer.

'I'll be goddamned,' Wendell repeated. 'Woodrow, you have just invented the poor man's acid dip!' He walked around the car, pushing it experimentally. By God! It *was* as light as it could get.

'Woodrow!' he said. 'Peewee! We're not licked yet! This car's going to run again! In fact, this car is going to run tomorrow, over in Atlanta!'

Woodrow started to protest. 'But, boss, there's not enough time – '

'Stop gabbing,' Wendell commanded. 'Hey, Peewee, look alive!'

Peewee snapped to attention. He was confused, but whatever Wendell wanted him to do, he'd do it.

'Go around the neighbourhood,' Wendell said, 'and get every man around here who knows anything about cars. Get them here fast! We've got a race car to build!'

Peewee took off down the driveway, saving his breath for the neighbors. He was going to be the Paul Revere of Danville.

Wendell was walking around the car, chuckling like a lunatic, when Mary came out to see what was happening. After Wendell told her his plan, she went back into the house to make coffee and lemonade. It looked like there'd be need for a lot of refreshments. Wendell, Jr., and Frankie were already out in the yard, and the littler girls, Kay and Sybil, had been put down for the night, so she collared Debbie and sent her to the store for cookies and doughnuts. Then the neighbors began to arrive, and the backyard took on a carnival air. Peewee had done his job well – it looked as if the whole county had gathered.

As it grew dark, the yard was lit by flashlights, lanterns, and even flares. Mary kept the coffee coming while the men – no one ever counted just how many there were – swarmed over the car. Wendell was everywhere at once, supervising, encouraging, and working like a fiend himself. It was dawn before the car was put together, with the radiator, transmission, and engine installed. It looked like hell, but it was together. Wendell announced, 'We've got ourselves a racer!'

He crawled into the car, and then the sound of the engine shook the windows of the house. So did the cheers. Wendell sent Wendell, Jr., and Frankie off to get buckets of whitewash and brushes. He himself painted the big 'thirty-four' on each side, and then he shook hands all around as half the county went home to get some sleep. Mary, worn to a frazzle, was grateful to see that the boys had finally collapsed. Wendell helped her carry the sleeping children to bed, then joined Woodrow and Peewee at the kitchen table for a last round of coffee.

Two hours later, at 7 a.m., the racer was hooked onto the Packard, and Wendell, Peewee, and Woodrow were on their way to Atlanta. Woodrow and Peewee were drowsy after the night's activities, but Wendell, at the wheel, was chipper as could be. 'Woodrow, wake up,' he said. 'You, too, Peewee.' He was answered by sleepy groans, but he went right on talking. 'Listen, you guys, I'm telling you. That car is really going to fly. Wait till you see the look on those jokers' faces when it just runs away and hides! They are just not going to believe it! Woodrow? Peewee?'

There was no response, and Wendell kept his thoughts to himself for a while. But halfway to Atlanta, a big semi, marked with the insignia of one of the factory teams, roared past the Packard, giving it a blast of horn. Wendell leaned out of the window to shout after it. 'Get it on while you can,' he yelled. 'Because once we get on the track, you aren't going to touch me!'

V

Atlanta was professional all the way – a paved and banked track, timed qualifying laps, safety inspections of the cars. Most important, it was the Grand National Series.

Wendell left Woodrow to manage the car through the tech inspection and went with Peewee to the concession stand. He wolfed down two doughnuts and was finishing a cup of what had to be the worst coffee he'd ever tasted when Bubba White joined them. The three men walked back together to have a look at Wendell's Chevrolet. Bubba was curious as could be about the accidental acid dip and wanted to see for himself.

As they approached the Chevrolet, they could see that Woodrow was excited about something. 'Look here, Wendell,' he said, indicating the rear tires. Wendell took one look and whistled softly.

'What's up, man?' Bubba asked. He was feeling the metal of the doors, marveling. They really did feel as thin as the factory cars.

'I just don't believe it,' Wendell said. 'Just look here! Some son of a bitch has cut my tires halfway through with a knife. Fixed them so they'd blow out while I was running.'

Bubba looked, and didn't like it. 'Yeah,' he said. 'Seems we've got ourselves a bunch of real jokers here today. And I'm not surprised. This is real reb country.' He pointed to the infield. 'Just look over there.'

They all looked to where Bubba was pointing. On the infield stood the remains of the charred cross.

'Yep,' Bubba went on, 'this is where they put on their white sheets and hold their meetings. Right here.'

Wendell shrugged, then kicked at one of the damaged tires.

'I got some extra tires, if you need them,' said Bubba. 'And it looks like you do.' He went off with Woodrow to get them.

Wendell was too tired to be furious. He'd been up all night working on the car, then there had been the long, hot drive to Atlanta, fighting heavy traffic a good part of the way. Now he wasn't going to allow any joker to keep him out of this important race. He'd get mad later – after he'd won! He looked up into the stands, which were nearly full. There was no colored grandstand any more, so people were pretty much mixed up. All the same, he knew who would be cheering him on.

Woodrow came back with the tires, and they went to work replacing the slashed ones. Peewee had gone back to the concession stand for coffee.

Wendell looked up to see Beau Welles standing by the car. 'Hey, boy,' Welles said, 'have some trouble with your tires?'

Wendell decided to ignore him. He wondered if Welles had been to the Klan meeting the night before. Could be, except that Welles wasn't from around Atlanta. Probably belonged to his own little Klavern someplace else.

'Boy,' Welles persisted, 'I'm talking to you. I got me two cars in this race, and I'm going to drive one of them right through you.'

Wendell sighed deeply and stood up. Welles was taller than he was, so he had to look up slightly to meet his eyes. Calmly and slowly, he said, 'Welles, you couldn't drive stars up a goat's ass.'

Welles's blue eyes seemed about to pop right out of his head. He took a second to regain his composure, then said evenly, 'Boy, you better watch out. There ain't nothing worse than a smart-ass nig –'

Wendell cut him short. 'Beau Welles, you're bigger than I am. But you just listen to one thing. You aren't any meaner than I am, and if you hit my car today, one of us is going to hell.'

Welles walked away, passing Peewee, who was returning with the coffee. 'What did he want?' asked Peewee.

'Not a thing,' said Wendell, and he went back to changing the tire.

Minutes later, Wendell drove out on the track for his

qualifying run. He knew right away that he'd like driving here. The tires bit nicely on the turns, and he realized that he was doing well. The new lightweight car felt better than any he'd ever driven before. Number Thirty-Four was doing just fine.

He didn't realize *how* well he'd done until he reached the pit. Peewee came running up with his stopwatch, half crazy with excitement. 'Man,' he shouted, 'your time was just sensational! I make out that you averaged more than a hundred and ten miles an hour! That's got to be good for something!'

It was good for the pole position – the first time Wendell had ever had the pole. Man, he thought, but that Chevy *is* something! He felt good as he crossed the infield to gather around the flag with the other drivers for the pre-race meeting. Bubba had qualified for the inside pole, next to him. They both heard one of the other drivers ask, 'Who got the poles for the feature?'

And they both heard Beau Welles answer, 'Two niggers.'

Bubba started out for Welles, but Wendell stopped him. 'You just let me handle this,' he said. 'Welles and me, we already had to have words once this afternoon.'

He walked over and poked his finger right into Welles's face. 'Boy,' he said deliberately, 'did you call me a nigger?'

'Take your finger out of my face,' Welles said.

'I just want you to remember,' Wendell said, 'that I already told you I'm not going to take one damn thing more from you – today or any other time.' He turned to the other drivers, who looked bored. 'I won the pole,' he announced, 'and if you don't think I deserved it, you just try and outrun me.'

The pre-race meeting got started then, and Wendell noticed that the other drivers, cool though they appeared to be, were at pains to keep him and Bubba at some distance from Welles. I made my point, he thought.

But he wasn't so sure when, on the pace lap, Welles pulled up alongside him. He couldn't hear over the noise of the cars, and it was hard to see, except out of the corner of his eye, but it looked to Wendell like Welles was pointing a menacing finger at his head.

Shit, he thought, I haven't got any time for this kind

of foolishness. He reached under the dashboard to the holster he had taped there, drew out the pistol, and pointed it straight at Welles's head. Welles dropped back so fast that the car behind him bumped him nearly off the track. Then the green flag dropped, and Wendell sailed right out in front of the pack.

The Chevy was still running well, and Wendell was out front for the first thirty laps. Then Tommy Gale, one of the new drivers, managed to slingshot him on the back straight. Wendell pulled into Gale's draft, planning to reverse the maneuver as soon as he could. Bubba pulled into Wendell's draft, and three other cars pulled up on Bubba, forming a six-car train that moved rapidly away from the rest of the pack.

Then Tommy Gale's engine blew, scattering metal and oil across the track. Tires screeched as the six lead cars began to spin out, bouncing off each other and off the retaining wall of the track. Wendell pulled sharply to the right and struck the wall almost head-on. He spun down toward the infield, piling up with Bubba on the way.

The emergency crews were there before the disabled cars had stopped moving. Wendell had been unconscious for only two minutes when they pulled him out of the wreckage of the Chevy. The crowd cheered wildly during the wreck and the clean-up operations. It was what they'd come to see.

VI

Bubba had been lucky; he had walked away from the wreck with only a few bruises. He and his wife Bobbi were waiting at the hospital when Mary and the boys arrived. Bubba didn't know what he was going to say to comfort Mary, but he thought maybe Bobbi would come up with something.

Bobbi and Mary hugged and kissed, and Bubba was relieved that Mary was not letting herself cry, even at Bobbi's words of sympathy. They all waited in silence until a nurse came into the room.

'Is he conscious yet?' Mary asked. 'When can we see him?'

'The doctor is with him now,' the nurse said. 'You'll be able to see him – well, pretty soon.' She vanished.

'No news is good news.' It was all Bubba could think of to say.

'No news is no news,' Mary said. Then she said what Bubba had hoped she wouldn't. 'Bubba, you're his friend. Can't you talk to him about doing something else?' She got up and walked to the window.

Bubba knew that nothing he or anyone else could say would ever change Wendell's mind about racing. He knew that Bobbi would never question his own devotion to it, that would never occur to her. But Bobbi was different from Mary. Back in the hills where Bobbi and he came from, women didn't ask questions of their men. He became aware of Mary's eyes on him.

'I can understand that you're upset,' Bubba said. 'But really, racing cars ain't such a bad life. Look at me, now. Hell, if I weren't doing this, where would I be? Back dirt farming on my daddy's old place? Clerking in some store for wages?'

Bubba, Mary thought, I surely do love you, but I can see that you're going to be no help at all. She jumped as the nurse stuck her head suddenly around the door.

'Mrs Scott?' the nurse said. 'You can go in now. But don't stay too long. He can't talk, anyhow – the doctor had to wire up that broken jaw.'

Frankie and Wendell, Jr., looked at each other and smiled. 'Broken jaw's not so bad,' Frankie said. 'It could have been a whole lot worse.' They followed Mary down the hall and into Wendell's room. Bubba and Bobbi brought up the rear, and the nurse tried to stop them at the door – the rule said only two visitors at a time, and three had already gotten right past her – but gave up fast when they just swept on through.

Mary looked down at Wendell. He was a mess, but she was relieved that he'd come away with only a broken jaw.

'Well, here we all are,' she said. 'Just like a family reunion. Looks like all it takes is just one little accident to bring family and friends together, just like at Christmas. Now, isn't this nice?'

Bubba looked at her with surprise. Bobbi would never take that tone with him, he thought – at least, not more than once.

Wendell mumbled something.

'Doctor says you've got a busted jaw,' Wendell, Jr. said. Wendell mumbled some more. He already knew all that.

'Which means no talking,' Mary said. 'Now, boys, you just scoot on outside for a couple of minutes. Your father and I are going to have a little conversation.'

'But he can't talk,' Frankie said.

'That's just the idea,' Mary said, with dangerous sweetness. 'Now, outside. Scoot.' They scooted.

Bubba picked up the cue. 'Me and the missus just dropped in to say hello, Wendell. Knew there wasn't anything wrong with you. Hell, a busted jaw might just be the best thing that's happened to you. Teach you to keep your fool mouth shut. Now, you take care, and as soon as you get back to Danville, Bobbi and me'll come around to see how you're doing.' Bobbi smiled as she followed him out of the room.

Mary closed the door behind them, then put her hands

on her hips and glared down at her husband. 'Now, Wendell,' she said firmly, 'I've been thinking about this for a long time, and I want you to give up racing.' He mumbled something. 'Shhh,' she said, 'the doctor said you weren't supposed to try to talk.' She sat down on the edge of the bed and took his hand.

'You set out to race,' Mary said, 'when everybody said it couldn't be done. And you did it. You went out and proved you could do it. You've won a lot of races, and everyone respects what you've done. You've proved your point.' She gave way suddenly to anger. 'Man, you've got to be some sort of a fool! You just won't quit! You're nearly forty years old, and look at you. Most of these new boys you're driving against have years on you. They've got the sponsors, the car companies, the oil companies, the money. They've got the best cars and the best mechanics, and you can't even pay old Woodrow a decent salary! And you, you haven't got a sponsor, and you'll probably never get one. And you just won't give up until you kill yourself, or some idiot like that Beau Welles does it for you! God knows he's been trying hard enough!'

Crying at last, Mary buried her face in his stomach.

'Wendell, I love you. And I don't want a dead hero. I want you alive. Please say you'll give it up.' She reached blindly for a handkerchief, mopped her face, then found an unbandaged part of his to kiss.

Wendell wanted to kiss her back, but the broken jaw made it impossible. Still he tried. He loved and respected this woman, and he wondered now if he had any right to risk making her a widow with five fatherless children.

Mary was getting herself back under control. 'You just get some rest now,' she said. 'I'll be back in a little while.' At the door she paused with her hand on the knob and looked back. 'Honey,' she said, 'don't pay any attention to what I just said. You know how I talk foolish sometimes.' She went out and closed the door behind her.

Wendell tried to put his thoughts in order. Maybe Mary was right, maybe it was time for him to quit. This accident had certainly given him something to think about, and the time to do the thinking. He'd been pretty lucky – a wonderful wife, five wonderful children. And he'd been able to live most of his life doing what he wanted to do, being around cars, fixing them, racing them, winning with them. But he'd just now made it to the Grand National circuit, and he still had to win a Grand National race. Winning one big race – that was his goal. He had to do it, even if it broke every bone in his body. Wendell almost grinned at that thought. In view of the fact that at that very moment he was flat on his back in a hospital bed. He wondered if anything remained of the Chevy. Better ask Bubba. It didn't seem like a good idea to ask Mary.

A week later, when he got out of the hospital, he learned that the racer had been completely destroyed.

VII

Wendell's mind was made up by the time he got back home to Danville – he would go for one big one. His problem was that he didn't have a car, not one good enough for the Grand National circuit. Cars cost money, and what money he had was for the kids' education. He wasn't going to touch that. And Mary was right, he *wasn't* getting any younger – and maybe soon he wouldn't be able to compete with drivers who were fifteen to twenty years his junior.

Fretting around the house one evening, Wendell wondered what ideas Bubba might have for raising cash. Bubba had said he'd talk to a man and then tell Wendell something he might want to hear about. Bubba and Bobbi were on their way over for supper – maybe there would be some word tonight.

When the Whites arrived, Bobbi went straight out to the kitchen to talk to Mary, but Bubba placed a jug of moonshine in Wendell's arms. Wendell filled two glasses, and Bubba raised his for a toast. 'Here's to two good old boys,' he said.

Wendell seconded the thought, and they got down to some serious drinking.

'All the boys miss you down at the track,' Bubba said.

'If all of them had missed me, I wouldn't have been in the hospital,' Wendell said, slapping his knee.

They reminisced for a while, and then Mary called them into the kitchen for supper, adding pointedly, '*If* you gentlemen are interested in anything besides racing.'

There was a good deal of food, and they gobbled it down, despite Mary's admonishments. 'No race going on here,' she said. 'No prizes for finishing first.'

'Bubba always eats real fast,' said Bobbi.

When the meal was finished, the women began to clear away and the men went back into the living room for some more conversation, washed down with moonshine.

They had broached a second bottle before Wendell got around to asking, trying to make it sound casual, 'Did you see that man you said you were going to see?'

'Yeah,' said Bubba. 'Glad you mentioned it. It nearly slipped my mind.'

It hadn't really, but he'd been mulling over whether or not it was as good an idea as it had seemed. Mary might well kill him for suggesting it, seeing how nervous she was about Wendell risking his neck.

'You see,' Bubba said slowly, 'I've been making me some extra money driving in thrill shows, a couple of nights a week, for a fellow named Flash Thompson. Do some rolls and a little T-bone number. And I asked Flash if he could fix it so you could do a little stunt or two, make yourself some money that way.'

Wendell leaned forward. 'What'd he say?'

'Fine by him,' Bubba replied. 'Now, how much money do you think you need to get back on the tracks?'

'About four thousand dollars,' Wendell said. 'And soon, if I want to get in that National race over in Jacksonville. If I don't qualify in that one, I don't get any money this year.'

'Four thousand!' Bubba whistled softly. 'Stunt driving doesn't pay all that well. I get seventy-five bucks a show for doing the T-bone. And the only thing that pays more is crashing the wall of ice.'

'How much is that?' Wendell asked.

'Two hundred dollars.'

'Okay,' Wendell said. 'Whatever it is, that's for me.' Looking toward the kitchen, he lowered his voice. 'Don't tell Mary, but I'm trying a demolition derby, too. I've got me a car that's good enough for that, and a guy called me yesterday to find out would I drive in one Saturday. What do you think?'

Bubba considered for a minute. 'Demo derby's not so bad,' he said. 'Why not do it? Just a lot of bammin' and frammin'. Go on, give it a go, and I'll talk to Thompson about you doing the wall of ice on Sunday.' He leaned forward, concerned. 'Hey, listen, Wendell, you do feel all right now, don't you?'

'All right?' said Wendell. 'Man, I never felt better.'

By the time Bobbi and Mary came into the living room to call the evening to an end, they were back to drinking to the good old days.

'To the Roanoke Volunteer Ambulance Service,' Wendell proposed. Even Bubba, who'd drink to the telephone book if anyone asked him to, looked dumbfounded. 'To the what?' he asked. Mary and Bobbi giggled.

'To the Roanoke Volunteer Ambulance Service,' Wendell repeated. 'Don't you remember, that time down in Roanoke when they wouldn't let me on the track until an ambulance from one of the black hospitals came to stand by, just in case I got in a wreck? My own private ambulance.'

Bubba remembered, and chuckled. 'Yeah! And when we finally got going, those two white drivers tangled, and then the white ambulance broke down, and they had to take them away in yours instead!'

The two men broke up laughing, for the hundredth time that evening.

'It's after midnight, boys,' Mary said.

'Bubba, I think I'd better drive home tonight,' Bobbi said. She got the car keys out of his pocket, and led him to the door.

'You take care now, Wendell,' Bubba said as he was towed out. 'I'll talk to old Flash first thing tomorrow.'

Mary turned to Wendell the moment the door was closed. 'Old Flash who? And talk to him about what?'

So it all came out. Wendell confessed not only about the thrill show, but also about the demolition derby. Mary was more understanding than he had expected, but it was clear that she didn't like either idea. He was surprised when she said she'd come along and watch Saturday night.

VIII

Mary brought the kids with her to the demolition derby Saturday night. Wendell had told the little girls not to get upset if they saw other cars slamming him around, because it was all for fun, and no one was going to get hurt. He hoped that Mary believed that, too, but he had a feeling that she didn't.

After only five minutes of sitting in the stands, Mary was already a little scared. The crowd was so wild that it made the normal stock car crowd look like a Chamber of Commerce meeting. And they were out for blood. Mary leaned forward as Wendell drove out onto the field in an old four-door Studebaker he'd fixed up. He joined a formation of about thirty other cars, in various states of decay, that faced each other in a rough circle at the center of the field. From where Mary sat, the other drivers all looked young – farm boys, she thought, or just in from the hills. They were all white, as was most of the crowd.

An official blew a whistle, jumped back off the track, and the derby was on. The cars charged at each other, and three or four of them dissolved on the spot. The crowd went wild. A man to Mary's left yelled, 'Kill 'em!' and a lady on her right screamed, 'Hit 'em harder! Smash 'em into the wall!' Mary wished she hadn't brought the children.

Down on the field, Wendell was having a high old time. He was taking an incredible pounding, but he was giving better than he got. He backed hard into a Ford, then hit a Chevrolet broadside, grinning all the time, enjoying every second. He tore into the pack with complete abandon, using his disintegrating Studebaker for all it was worth. A back door fell off, but he didn't miss it. Everyone was going every possible direction, all over the track, and every single car was fair game. Wendell ran joyfully right through a Chrysler. Too bad Beau Welles isn't out here, he thought, so he could see how he liked it, with *everybody* playing his way.

After about twenty minutes of mayhem, there were only two cars left alive, Wendell's Studebaker and a big blue Buick. They circled each other warily, hunting among the wreckage that had been twenty-eight other cars, looking for an opening. Wendell moved away from the center of the track, and the Buick came right after him. The crowd yelled louder – it looked like the Studebaker was running away. Then Wendell did two of his fast bootlegger's turns and rammed the Buick with his rear end. He connected with the radiator, and the Buick sputtered and died, emitting great puffs of steam. The crowd went crazy. Wendell climbed out of what was left of the Studebaker, took the checkered flag from the official, and waved it at his family.

Mary waved back, then sank down onto the hard bench and let her stomach settle. The kids were excited and happy, the littlest most of all, as far as she could tell. As she herded them toward the exit, Debbie chatted happily about the *next* demolition derby, and Mary didn't tell her that there wasn't going to *be* another one, not if she had anything to say about it.

They collected Wendell, who was still elated by the good time he'd had, and drove home. Mary put the kids to bed while he had a hot bath. Then she laid down the law, and extracted his promise that there would be no more demolition derby foolishness, or anything like it. Except for Flash Thompson's thrill show, out at the fairgrounds, the next night. Arrangements had been set there for Wendell to do the wall-of-ice stunt.

The kids were still excited Sunday morning, what with the demolition derby they'd just seen and the thrill show coming up. It was like having Christmas two days running. Mary thought she might have to tie them down to make them finish eating their breakfasts. The boys spent the afternoon helping Wendell hitch one of his old racers, the old red Plymouth, to the family car, and even touched up the 'thirty-four' painted on its sides. The three girls contented themselves with staying underfoot all day. By dinnertime Mary had given up completely, and when it was finally time to go out to the fairgrounds, she was relieved – though she wasn't exactly looking forward to the show.

Word had gotten around that Wendell Scott was going to do something risky that evening, and there was heavy traffic going out to the fairgrounds. Wendell had to endure ten minutes of bumper-to-bumper traffic inching along before he was able to pull up in front of the main gate and let his family out. Mary kissed him, and the boys shook his hand. It was the first time they'd ever done that, and he wondered if helping on the Plymouth that afternoon had made them feel suddenly grown up and important.

As he drove around to the back of the stadium, a lot of people, black and white, waved to him and wished him luck. As far as a lot of this crowd were concerned, he'd put Danville on the map, and they were grateful. The security guard recognized him, too, said 'Good evening, Mr Scott,' and waved him right on through.

Sitting with Bobbi White in the stands, Mary watched Wendell unhook the Plymouth and saw Bubba walk over to talk to him. Bobbi was carrying on about Bubba's stunt. It was so pretty, she told Mary, that it gave her the shivers. Mary wondered what it could be. She told the kids to sit quiet in their seats and watch the show. Right now it was just three girls in bathing suits being paraded around the track, standing on the roofs of three cars, holding on by ropes. Announcements were being made over the loudspeaker, but they were hard to hear, since every one of the dozen drivers in the infield was revving his motor. The kids were bored and began wriggling around. It was clear that this show wasn't going to be as much fun as a demolition derby. They perked up, though, at the first of the real stunts, and they became downright rambunctious as one car after another shot off a ramp and into space, landing far from the launching point.

Down on the field, Wendell looked around. He recognized a lot of Thompson's drivers; they were old stock car racers who had begun in the sport when Bubba and he had. He hadn't seen them for years, which meant that they were no longer racing.

Bubba came over, fastening his helmet. Behind him on the field, men were rolling around ramps and cars, setting up for his stunt. 'Now, you just watch this, Wendell,' he said. 'You've never seen anything so pretty.'

'You take care,' Wendell said.

Bubba got into his old Ford and revved up the engine. 'Only thing about this trick is that it sure does use up cars,' he said.

The crowd fell silent as the loudspeaker blared: 'And now ladies and gentlemen, presenting one of the most dangerous, most breathtaking, most hellacious stunts ever performed by mortal man – Bubba White and the incredible T-bone smash!'

Bubba gunned up his engine three or four more times as the crowd – every man, woman, and child – leaned forward in anticipation. Slowly, Bubba headed across the field, taking his time. Then he popped his clutch and went full out for the ramp. He ran up the ramp and off the end, sailing into the air. The Ford turned itself nose down and landed right on the target, a parked jalopy. It came to rest perfectly perpendicular, its nose stuck right down through the wreck's roof. A perfect T-bone!

Up in the stands, Bobbi was babbling with pleasure, and Mary was just opening her eyes. She looked at the wreckage and couldn't see Bubba. Bobbi didn't seem worried, but Mary was scared to death. At last she saw Bubba crawl up through the back window of the Ford and climb down over what was left of the jalopy. He was waving nonchalantly to the crowd, who whooped and cheered back. Mary wondered what in God's name Wendell was supposed to be doing here. The kids were chattering on about how they couldn't wait to see their daddy. She could wait.

'How do you like the show so far?' Bobbi asked.

'Bobbi,' she said, 'I just hope that Wendell finds some easier way to get some money. Maybe we should think about selling the house.'

Bobbi just laughed and patted her hand. 'You'll get used to it.'

Mary felt Wendell, Jr.'s, elbow in her ribs and looked out on the field to where he was pointing. She saw a full-sized truck dragging a huge wall of ice. It must have been ten feet tall. Dear God, she thought, don't tell me Wendell's going to have to run over, under, or through that.

Wendell was getting his own first look at the ice wall. And Bubba was telling him what to do. 'The important thing,' Bubba was saying, 'is to hit it right spang in the middle. When you're coming at it, at speed, it'll all look pretty much the same. But stay to the center, and when you get close enough, you'll see a piece of black cloth stuffed in between the blocks. There's some wood between the blocks there, so they don't melt together. And that's where you hit it. Okay?'

Wendell realized suddenly that though the stunt was genuinely dangerous, it depended at least partly on illusion. What looked from a distance like a wall of solid ice was in fact made up of blocks that would fall apart if the wall was hit dead center. But it had to be dead center. It was dead center or dead Scott, Wendell thought. He got into the Plymouth and started the engine, trying not to hear the announcer's voice.

'And now your attention, please!' the announcer said. 'Flash Thompson's Thrill Show has a real treat for you tonight, ladies and gentlemen! The noted colored racing driver Wendell Scott is here today, and will be performing the most dangerous stunt in automotive history. He will drive his high-powered racer full speed into a three-ton wall of ice. That's right, ladies and gentlemen, three tons! One mistake, one miscalculation, could be fatal! Here he comes now, so let's have a big hand for Wendell Scott!'

The crowd started screaming as Wendell circled the track, gaining speed. They were on their feet as he approached the wall of ice – even Mary, who wasn't sure that her legs were going to hold her up. The crowd's screams increased in volume as Wendell aimed the Plymouth at the wall of ice, and went right through, sending ice flying in all directions.

Mary sank back down as Wendell pulled himself out of the stove-in racer and waved to the crowd. She couldn't believe he was still in one piece. No more, she vowed to herself. No matter what it took, there'd be no more demolition derbies and no more thrill shows. Not ever! She began rounding up the kids.

'There now, wasn't that exciting? Didn't you just love it?' Bobbi asked.

Mary pretended that she hadn't heard the question.

IX

Coming out of the bank the next day, a little depressed after looking over his bank balance, Wendell ran into Sheriff Cotten. He hadn't seen the sheriff for some time – the last time he'd come around to the house, little Kay had asked if he had a warrant and then slammed the door in his face.

'How you doing?' Cotten greeted him, holding out his hand, which Wendell shook.

'You look fine,' said Cotten. 'Say, I read about your wreck down in Atlanta, and I'd say you were lucky to be walking around.'

Wendell just nodded.

'You going to run down in Jacksonville next month? We're all expecting you to win a Grand National one of these days.'

'Way things are going,' Wendell said, 'I don't even figure on getting on the track at Jacksonville, let alone winning.'

Cotten saw for the first time that Wendell looked troubled. 'Why? What's the matter?' he asked.

'My car's so tore up I can't run it anywhere, and I can't see my way clear to raising enough money to build me another one,' Wendell told him.

'Now, look here, Wendell,' Cotten said slowly. 'You and I may have had our differences in the past, but I hope you know it was nothing personal. It's just that I had a sworn job to do, and every time I turned around, there you were. But I'm not going to be sheriff much longer. Matter of fact, I'm running for mayor.' He waved toward a nearby telephone pole, on which Wendell saw a 'Cotten For Mayor' poster. 'Seems to me that DuPree's been in office long enough, and I thought I'd just take him on myself.'

Wendell wondered why Cotten was telling him all this. After all, in Danville, politics was still pretty much a matter for white folks only.

'Look here,' Cotten went on. 'Why don't you give me a call tomorrow? Maybe I can be of some help.'

'Thanks, Sheriff,' Wendell said. 'I will.' He watched the sheriff walk off, wondering what Cotten wanted from him.

Cotten wondered, too, as he drove away. He'd always genuinely liked Scott, or at least borne him no malice, and with the Federal people nosing around to make sure that black voters got registered, supporting a popular black hero wouldn't do him any harm. He'd have to talk to his supporters about it, see if there were some way to get Scott some money and himself some publicity that would help with the colored vote. This looked like it might be an election in which that vote might count for something.

Though neither Cotten nor Wendell knew it, Peewee had already hatched a plan that would help them both. He got to the Scott house just as Wendell got home from the bank, and, noticing that his friend looked glum, broke the news fast. 'Hey, man. Your troubles are over!'

Right then and there, on the front porch, Peewee told him all about the Great Wendell Scott Benefit. Wendell wasn't sure he much liked the idea – it sounded awfully close to charity – but by the time Mary had got them both sitting down at the kitchen table over coffee, he had realized there was no point in arguing. Peewee could not be stopped – the Wendell Scott Benefit was going to be held, with or without Wendell Scott.

'Okay,' Wendell finally agreed. 'Just don't go and get carried away by things.'

'Don't worry. You just leave everything – and I do mean everything – to me.' Peewee stood up and patted Wendell on the shoulder. 'See you later, man. I've got to get over to Sweets'. I'll get some of the boys together, and we'll plan out – let's see – some speeches, and some liquor, and some food, and some live entertainment. All you got to do, Mary, you and Wendell, is just sit and be the guests of honor.'

'If there's going to be anything you have to clear with

the cops,' Wendell said, 'then call up Sheriff Cotten. I was just talking to him and it seems like he wants to do something to help.'

'I'm going to call him up right now!' Peewee was half-way to the door before he remembered his manners. 'Thank you for the coffee, Mary,' he said. 'See you around, Wendell.'

Wendell and Mary looked at each other. 'I still don't like it much,' he said. 'But you might as well try to stop a freight train as try to stop old Peewee when he gets an idea.'

He wondered how Mary would like Sweets', since they were both going to be guests of honor. She'd never set foot in the place, and he'd just as soon she didn't start.

'I don't see how it's going to hurt you any,' Mary said. 'All you've got to do is just sit there while people give speeches about you. After demolition derbies and thrill shows, that doesn't seem like much. But you know,' she went on, teasing, 'from everything I've heard about Sweets', maybe it won't be any less dangerous.'

'Honey,' said Wendell, teasing her back, 'whatever you've heard, you can't know the half of it.' For the first time in years, he found himself thinking about Luanne and Alma. Hell, he thought, they've most likely got grand-children by now.

Peewee was back before suppertime, and he had a lot to report. He handed Wendell a flyer announcing the One-Time-Only Wendell Scott Benefit Jamboree, to be held at Sweets' Café, November 15th, 1964, Come One Come All. Wendell fingered the advertisement and discovered that the ink was dry. He'd been right – Peewee had planned to go ahead with this thing, with or without him, and it looked as if it had been planned some time ago.

'Looks good, doesn't it?' Peewee asked, wondering if Wendell was going to notice that the flyer wasn't exactly hot off the press. He went on fast. 'Sweets' is going to donate the cook and the food. And those guys up in the hills are going to donate the moonshine. Doesn't that beat all?'

'Moonshine?' Wendell asked.

'Everything's cool with the cops, man,' Peewee assured

him. 'I talked to Sheriff Cotten and you know what? Cotten's going to make a speech.'

'We don't want this to be a political rally,' Wendell said.

'Cotten just wants to show his face and say a few words,' Peewee said. 'And he promised he'd leave right afterward. So I put him down first on the list,' he added, suddenly practical. 'And besides, he took a whole bunch of tickets to sell to his friends, and there's no danger of any of them showing up at all.'

'Peewee,' said Wendell, returning to the flyer. 'Just when did you have these things printed up?'

'Yesterday,' Peewee confessed. He had the grace to look abashed, and Wendell decided not to ride him.

'Got to run,' Peewee said, backing toward the door. 'There's still a million details to see to. So long.' He was gone.

Over supper, Wendell told Mary all about the Jamboree. The kids couldn't go to it, she said. She didn't want any of her kids to be hanging around Sweets'.

'November fifteenth's only five days away,' Frankie said.

'Peewee works fast,' Wendell told him. He began to be nervous. He didn't know about facing all those people without having a car around him.

X

The Benefit Jamboree was a big success, and even Wendell finally relaxed and had a good time. People turned out from as far away as Roanoke and Lynchburg. Sheriff Cotten made a nice, short speech and went away after shaking a lot of black hands. It had been a good evening for him, too. Best of all, when Wendell and Peewee went into the sheriff's office to count up the proceeds, they were only forty dollars short of their goal. And then Sweets himself added the forty.

The next day Wendell went out and bought a big blue Ford, and drove it straight through the black section of Danville, waving and smiling. He went out of his way to pass the 'Cotten for Mayor' headquarters on Main Street and parked at the curb until Cotten came out to shake his hand. Then he went home and got down to business. The Jacksonville race was scheduled for December 1st, so he and Woodrow had lots of work to do. It was going to be the last Grand National race of the season, and Florida was a good piece away.

Wendell, Jr. and Frankie helped out when they got home from school – Mary was firm about their not taking any days off 'sick' – and Woodrow and Wendell worked pretty much around the clock every day, except for Thanksgiving. Mary insisted that they come in to the table for Thanksgiving dinner, but they were back out in the yard within the hour. It was the fastest holiday meal Mary could remember. The last weekend before the race, she resigned herself to feeding her family sandwiches. It was hard on everyone, but by the last day of November, Wendell had himself a racing car he was proud of.

Woodrow helped him load the car onto its trailer and hook the trailer to the Packard. It was going to be a long drive, and they would have to get an early start. The Packard, by now overhauled a number of times, was going to be especially crowded, since this time Wendell, Jr. and Frankie were going along to help out in the pit. Wendell remembered other trips in the Packard and wondered how Woodrow was going to make out on this one. On most of those other trips, the big man had slept most of the way, taking up the whole back seat. Hell, Wendell thought, I guess we can always make Peewee ride in the glove compartment. Smiling at the memory of the old joke, he walked around the Ford to admire it a little more. He patted the big white 'Thirty-Four' on its side. It was pretty, just as pretty as any of the big factory cars.

When Peewee and Woodrow drove up at dawn, he was ready. He yelled for the boys to come, kissed Mary and the girls goodbye, then took his place in the Packard and settled down for a nap. Woodrow drove. They left Danville in the early-morning quiet, heading south. Traffic was light, and at Greenboro Woodrow gave up the wheel to Peewee, moved into the back seat and, sitting bolt upright, began almost instantly to snore. At Columbia, after they'd all had some coffee, Wendell took over the driving. It was beginning to get hot.

Nobody talked much. The men had been through too many races together to have need of it. Once in a while, Peewee would tell the boys some kind of race story, but Wendell, Jr. and Frankie had heard most of them before. The time for stories was after a race, Wendell thought, drinking with your friends. They reached the Jacksonville city limits sign, and then there seemed to be a sign directing them to the speedway about every two blocks.

It was hot as hell when they parked on the speedway infield and got out to stretch their legs. Qualifying was about to start, and when they had unloaded the car, Woodrow and Wendell began checking it over one final time.

Peewee disappeared, then came back with a Jacksonville newspaper. 'Hey, Wendell,' he said, 'it doesn't look as though you're favored to win today. Fact is, I can't find your name anywhere in this piece on the race.'

Wendell, Jr. and Frankie grabbed the paper and looked, too, with no better result. 'Doesn't matter,' said Wendell. 'I'm here, whether it's in the paper or not.'

'Well, you better win today, Scott,' said Peewee. 'It's

so hot, I never want to come back here again. In fact' – he adapted an old joke – 'if someone was to give me both Hell and Jacksonville, I'd live in Hell and rent out Jacksonville.'

Peewee laughed along with the rest of them, and then suddenly he stopped. 'Don't look now, Wendell,' he said, 'but here comes trouble.'

Beau Welles, strolling by, had halted to look at the Ford. He turned to Wendell. 'Hey, Scott,' he said, 'I see you ain't got a sponsor yet. Matter of fact, someone told me you're so bad off that you tried to get the government to sponsor you on welfare.'

Wendell zipped up his uniform jacket. 'Talk to me out there on the track,' he said, 'where it counts.'

Welles was already moving away, and Wendell addressed his sons, who looked as if they were going to follow him. 'Now, you just stay cool,' he said.

This time it was Woodrow who came up with a joke to make them all feel better. 'Okay, Wendell,' he said, 'car's as good as I can get her. Now do you want me to find the Hoo-Doo man?'

Wendell explained to the boys. 'I guess I never told you about Woodrow and the Hoo-Doo man. It was up at Martinsville, and Woodrow found this old guy who claimed he was some kind of witch doctor or something. He went around putting little marks on all the other cars and saying spells.'

Wendell, Jr. asked the right question. 'What happened?'

'All the cars finished except me,' Wendell said. 'I blew my engine on the very first lap.' Still laughing, he pulled on his helmet, crawled through the Ford's window, and went out on the track for his qualifying run.

Bubba had joined the group by the pit by the time he came back off the track. They shook hands and exchanged gossip for a minute, and then Bubba went off to qualify. Wendell waited for the qualifying results to be announced. When he heard them, he shook hands with Woodrow, Peewee, and his sons, and headed for his starting position, which was on the outside of the third row. It wasn't bad, but it could have been better. Beau Welles had qualified fifth and would be right beside him.

XI

Wendell began moving out just as soon as the green flag dropped. He knew that he was up against the best drivers in the country. That felt good, and so did his car. He was in contention all the way, and he knew it. After thirty laps he was in sixth place. Woodrow signaled him for a pit stop, gassed the Ford up, and changed the tires on the right side in no time flat, and Wendell was back out on the asphalt again.

He did not fall below sixth place for the first hundred laps of the two-hundred-lap race. Then he began to move up. When he made his third pit stop on the hundred-and-third lap, he was in third place. Wendell gave Woodrow and the boys a big 'thumbs up' signal as he hit the track again.

It was then that Wendell, Jr. noticed that Number Thirty-Four was no longer posted on the scoreboard. He ran over to Peewee and pointed out what was happening. 'Goddamn it,' Peewee yelled over the noise, 'What's wrong here! Where's Wendell's number!'

They forgot about it as they watched Wendell move into second place, right behind Beau Welles. They didn't even notice that the public-address announcements were no longer mentioning Wendell Scott's name or number. As far as the race officials were concerned, Wendell seemed to have vanished right off the face of the earth. And what with all the cars lapping each other on the track again and again, only the sharpest-eyed fan could have told that Wendell was right up there in second place.

Second place took Wendell himself a little by surprise. He couldn't quite credit his eyes when he glanced at the pit and saw Woodrow holding up a sign that said 'P 2', while Frankie danced around with a chalkboard that read

'L-25'. Goddamn, Wendell thought, I knew I was doing well, but not that well! With twenty-five laps to go, it was time now to really stand on it.

Wendell pulled up as close as he could behind Welles, riding along in his draft. He bided his time, drifting along in the slipstream, until just the right moment. With fifteen laps to go, he pulled out beside Welles, and they went into a corner side by side. Welles didn't budge an inch, but Wendell eased by him and took the lead.

'He's running first!' Wendell, Jr. shouted.

'Damn announcer hasn't said a word about it!' Peewee shouted back. 'They must be dead up there in that officials' booth. Scoreboard doesn't show a damn thing!'

Frankie held up the pit board as Number Thirty-Four passed. It showed two laps to go. Woodrow did some figuring and decided that the fuel would hold, although they'd cut it real close.

Now the last lap, and Wendell was smiling. The race was over – and he'd won. He looked for the checkered flag, but didn't see it. He did another lap, still out in front, and still the flag didn't drop. What the hell was going on? he wondered. After two extra laps, the official finally dropped the checker, and Wendell brought the Ford to a stop in his pit. His sons practically dragged him out of the window in their jubilation, and Woodrow pounded him joyfully on the back.

Only Peewee stood aside, looking worried. He was listening hard. There had been no announcement of the winner yet.

Bubba came over. 'What the hell's going on?' he asked Wendell. 'How come there's no announcement yet? And hey, you tell me, wasn't that race a little long?'

Wendell nodded. He had a kind of sinking feeling, and he didn't want to talk just then, not even to Bubba. The crowd grew silent – everyone in the stadium was waiting to hear who had won.

The winner's name went on the scoreboard at the same moment it came over the loudspeaker – Beau Welles.

Wendell slammed his helmet down on the ground and headed off to the pit lane, ready to kill. He stormed up to the track officials, looking as dangerous as he felt. 'I want to register a protest,' he said. 'I won this race, and you all know I won it!'

Bubba came up behind him and put a hand on his arm. The officials all turned away, except for one, a little man with glasses, who looked up at Wendell and said, 'We'll look into it, we'll investigate, you just wait right here.' Then he scuttled off after his associates.

Bubba walked Wendell back to his car. Wendell, Jr., Frankie, Woodrow, and Peewee looked as if it were the end of the world. They all watched Beau Welles drive his car into Victory Lane.

Beau got out of his car and walked up to the winner's stand, waving every step of the way. Wendell saw the sun glint on the big golden trophy, and clenched his fists hard as a white-haired man in a seersucker suit presented it to Beau Welles. He felt like crying, and would not let himself look at his sons.

Beau Welles made a little thank-you speech, and Wendell heard a lot more of it than he wanted to. Welles thanked just about everyone for his win – his mother, his father, his wife, his children, his pit crew, his loyal fans, his sponsors, his country, and his God. Everybody but the family dog, Wendell thought, when he really should be thanking those goddamn officials!

A tall blonde climbed up on the winner's stand, wiggling her fanny, and Welles gave her a big kiss. Jesus Christ! thought Wendell, no wonder they didn't want me to win. The announcer asked the crowd to give Miss Jacksonville of 1964 a big hand, and for one wild minute Wendell wondered what it would have been like if it had been him up there. If he'd even just shaken her hand in front of that crowd, he'd have risked being torn limb from limb. A bunch of photographers moved in close to record Beau Welles embracing the trophy.

That really got to Wendell. He didn't want to be kissed by any beauty queen, but he damned well wanted that trophy, and the money that went with it. And he wanted the record books to show that on December 1st, 1964, Wendell Oliver Scott had won the Grand National race at Jacksonville, Florida.

'Hell, we'll protest, man!' Bubba said. 'And if they turn

down the protest, we'll take it right up to the president of NASCAR!'

Wendell liked Bubba's 'we', but he knew he had to fight this one out for himself. 'You go on, Bubba,' he said. 'Bobbi'll be waiting for you.' He motioned Peewee away from him, too, and the little man got the message. 'Hey, Wendell,' he said, 'me and Woodrow's going to have a few beers. Meet you right back here in a while.'

At the winner's stand, Wendell cornered the first official he found, the little man with the glasses.

'Look,' Wendell said, grabbing his arm, 'I know this is a mistake, and you know this is a mistake, and I'm not moving one inch until this mess is straightened out.'

'We're looking into it,' the man with the glasses said. 'You just stay calm, and someone will get right back to you. Don't worry.'

Wendell went back and joined his sons leaning against the car. They watched as the stands emptied out and as the grounds crew came out to clean up after the race. The other drivers were loading up their equipment and departing, but Wendell didn't move. He was ready to wait right there till next season if he had to.

Bubba, with Bobbi beside him, drove by in his tow car. 'Hang in there, man!' he yelled out the window. 'We all know you won!' Bobbi gave Wendell one of her toothpaste-ad smiles and waved cheerfully. Wendell didn't wave back.

It was beginning to get dark. Peewee and Woodrow came back across the infield. 'The beer tasted lousy,' Peewee explained, 'so we came back to wait alongside of you.'

'How long you going to wait?' Woodrow inquired.

'As long as it takes,' said Wendell.

'Thought so,' said Woodrow. He made himself comfortable against the Packard.

Wendell looked up to where lights were burning in the scoring tower. He wondered how long it was going to take them. He felt like a man turned to stone. After the joy of winning, and the humiliation of being cheated of his win, he didn't seem to have much emotion left. Just patience. At least the evening was turning cool, and that felt good after the heat of the day.

It was good and dark before he saw the white-haired

man in the seersucker suit approaching, a piece of paper in his hand.

'Mr Scott?' The man offered his hand, but Wendell didn't take it. 'Mr Scott, it seems you were right. You did win, after all. Congratulations!'

All of Wendell's anger returned, but he could not speak.

The official went on, trying to sound friendly. 'It seems the scorer made an error on your last pit stop. We're terribly sorry. Nothing like this has ever happened before, but' – he was getting nervous – 'like they say, nobody's perfect!'

Wendell just stared at him.

The official offered the piece of paper. 'Here. Here's the check for first-place money. I'm sorry that it took so long, but . . . well, better late than never.'

Peewee reached out and took the check, and the official turned to go.

Suddenly, Wendell moved. He grabbed the official by the arm and spun him around. 'Wait just a minute!' he shouted. 'What do you mean, with this "nobody's perfect, better late than never" shit?'

The white-haired man tried to remain calm. 'Look, Mr Scott,' he said, 'there's no need to get mad. We've acknowledged our mistake, and we've rectified it. The check's good.' He tried to turn away, but Wendell held him tightly. 'Please, Mr Scott,' he said, 'you're hurting me.'

'I'm hurting *you*?' Wendell shouted. '*I'm* hurting *you*? Where the hell's my trophy, man? Where's the beauty queen? Where's the reporters?'

'Please, Mr Scott,' the official said. 'The young lady has gone home. And the reporters left a long time ago – they couldn't be expected to wait around. And I'm sure Beau Welles will give you the trophy as soon as he learns what happened.'

Wendell pushed the man away. 'What?' he shouted. 'He'll do what?' He felt suddenly tired of it all. 'Get out of here! You just get the hell out of here! You just play your damn games! You think you can get away with murder because there's all of you and only one of me!'

The official recovered his footing. 'Mr Scott,' he said huffily, 'if you have any further statements on this matter, you can take it up with the executive board at Daytona. Good night.'

Wendell, Jr., spoke up for the first time in hours. 'Dad, this place stinks. Let's go home.'

'Yeah, you've got something there,' Wendell said. He put an arm around each of his sons. 'Let's go home.'